# Hitched

*Volume 3*

Kendall Ryan

# About the Book

I've ruined everything. I've broken the cardinal rule and fallen in love with my fake wife, and then I went and did the worst thing a husband can do.

Winning her back will be nearly impossible, but I've never backed down from a challenge before and I'm sure as hell not about to start now. Olivia will be mine, and I can't wait to put a bun in her oven.

You won't want to miss the final installment in Noah and Olivia's love story, and especially the way this over-the-top alpha male wins over his bride once and for all.

# Praise for *Hitched*

"I'm literally in love with *Hitched*. The irreverent humor, fun storyline and intriguing characters enchanted me immediately and I was hooked. I mean really, when a book has a chapter with only the two words being "Game on" (right after the chapter where Noah pulls his big boy parts out in a swanky bar) you know this is going to be a fun and funny read! And Ms. Ryan didn't disappoint . . . she kept me cracking up the entire read! I'm salivating for the next installment!" — *The Romance Reviews*

"Fun, flirty and steamy, *Hitched* will have you addicted from the first word! Kendall Ryan delivered big time, I'm practically salivating for more!" —*Angie and Jessica's Dreamy Reads*

"Kendall Ryan strikes gold in her latest super star, *Hitched*, a romantic comedy spiked with steam, anchored by angst, and flooded with feelings." —*Bookalicious Babes Blog*

"Charming, swoony and playful, Kendall Ryan's *Hitched* left me salivating for more. More Noah, more Olivia, more of this series which already has my heart all aflutter, my smile perma-pinned to my face, and my mind aching for answers." —*Give Me Books*

"*Hitched* was a perfect non-stop read! I read it in one sitting, and laughed so many times my belly ached. It's a fun, romantic read with a light-hearted story that made me ache for more when I finished." —*Jacqueline's Reads*

"*Hitched* will grab you hook, line, and sinker from the very first page. Olivia is a little bratty and Noah is a whole lot cocky but that dynamic makes for a sexual tension that I can tell is going to explode in the next two installments. And while this isn't your typical friends-to-lovers type of story, the shared history between the two adds a surprising depth. The steam level is heating up and once you pick it up, you won't want to put it down." —*Love Between the Sheets*

# Chapter One

*Olivia*

The feelings I'm developing for my new husband have startled me in their depth and intensity. Our marriage was only supposed to be a legal agreement—a business arrangement meant to appease the stakeholders. But we've quickly become something much more.

I stretch my arms overhead and let out a soft sigh. His vacated side of the bed is still warm and I roll over, soaking up the remnants of his body heat.

Sometimes I can still hardly believe it. I feel like a new Olivia, relaxed and fun and optimistic. The silly smile perma-fixed to my lips? It's crazy. Of course, it could be because Noah is thoughtful and kind and generous in bed . . . and hung like a damn elephant. That last part is just icing on the cake. I almost giggle.

If I have to be fake-married to anyone, I'm glad it's Noah. These last few weeks, we've really bonded, grown closer than I ever thought possible. I trust him, depend on him, and have finally started to let my icy exterior melt a little. And did I mention the great sex?

Speaking of sex, though . . . *God, where is he?* He was supposed to be getting a condom from the bathroom, but that should have taken about forty-five seconds, and I've been waiting forever for him to come back and ravish me.

With an impatient huff, I swing my legs over the side of our enormous bed and pad barefoot and naked down the hall. The bathroom door is mostly closed, but I give it a gentle nudge and it swings open.

Noah is standing in front of the sink, stark naked. A condom packet in one hand. A small but sharp-looking silver needle in the other.

*What the fuck?*

I don't even notice I've gasped until his head jerks up.

My heart plummets.

Noah's skin is pale and he stares at me with wide,

almost wild eyes. Does his expression come from guilt, or is he just startled and confused? I don't know which is worse.

I recoil back into the hall, my hand pressed to my mouth. *No, no, no . . .*

He looks down blankly at what's in his hands, as if he has no idea how those things got there, then hurls it all into the sink like it's burned him. "Olivia . . . w-wait, it's not, I wasn't . . ." he calls.

But I'm already running away, my breath tearing from my throat in sobs.

Not even five minutes ago, he was talking about how good it would feel to fuck me bare. Trying to tempt me into going without a condom. I thought he just wanted the intimacy—to get closer to me, to join together without barriers, skin on skin. But he was after something else. And when he couldn't convince me to give it to him . . . he was going to take it.

*What in the ever-loving hell is going on?*

Everything has suddenly clicked into horrible clarity. This explains why he's seemed subtly off—

sometimes restless, sometimes a little too still—ever since we dealt with Brad. I sensed something but I couldn't put my finger on the feeling, so I dismissed it as me being paranoid and reading too much into meaningless stuff. I figured he was probably just stressed from work and worried about the company's future.

Turns out my gut instincts were right all along. He was lying to me. And not just any old lie . . . he was trying to put a baby in me whether I wanted one or not. I shudder, thinking how close I came to disaster. If I hadn't barged into the bathroom just now, if I'd waited even one more minute . . .

But why in God's name would he even do this? The Noah I know is hardly a family man, dying to settle down and have kids.

Then again, I obviously don't know him as well as I thought I did.

I rush to the bedroom and yank on the first clothes I see—the sundress I wore to the spa today, the sundress Noah just peeled me out of. I need to cover myself up. My nudity suddenly isn't sexy or intimate anymore. I'm just *exposed*, and I can't be naked in front of a stranger.

His footsteps come close behind me. "Snowflake, let me explain."

"Get away from me!" My voice cracks into a near shriek. I hate the sound of it, hate how upset I am, how much power Noah has over my emotions. I want to roar, not whimper. "What the hell is wrong with you? Are you out of your fucking mind? What explanation could you possibly have for . . . for doing *that?*"

"I wasn't actually going to do it." Noah grimaces as the words rush out, like they scrape his throat coming up.

"Do what? Secretly poke a hole in your condom so you could sneak your fucking sperm into my uterus? Because that really seems like what you were doing!"

"Will you just listen to me for a minute? I only considered it because I was desperate. And I hate that the thought even crossed my mind. I could never actually—"

"Why were you desperate? What the hell are you

talking about?"

I need answers. All of them. Right the fuck now. And all he's giving me is nonsense babbling.

With a heavy sigh, Noah rakes his hand through his hair. He looks bitterly angry, but not at me—his expression is turned inward.

"Come with me. You need to see something . . . something I should have showed you a long time ago." He pulls on a pair of drawstring pants, seemingly not wanting to be naked any more than I do.

Noah offers his hand but I don't take it. I don't want to touch him right now. After waiting a moment, he lets his arm drop and turns away.

I follow him to the living room, where he picks up his briefcase leaning by the armchair. As he flicks through its tabbed folders, he asks, "You'd do anything to save this company, right?"

I furrow my brow in irritated confusion. "Of course I would. But what's that got to do with you trying to knock me up?"

He finds the file he wants, flips it to the second-to-last page, and thrusts it into my hands. "Here. Read this section."

I recognize this document. It's the inheritance contract we signed on our wedding day. "Why are you showing me something I already read? I know what it says."

"No, you don't, or we wouldn't be having this conversation right now." Noah points again at the section he wants me to see.

With a quiet huff, I start reading below his finger, skimming faster and faster and I grow more annoyed.

And then I see what Noah is talking about.

*After being wed, Noah Tate and Olivia Cane agree to consummate their marriage and produce an heir. The resulting pregnancy should occur within ninety days of this executed agreement.*

My heart stops. "W-we have to produce an heir?" I yell.

Noah nods grimly. "Our inheritance isn't final until

we have a baby, or at least until we show a positive pregnancy test as proof that one is on the way. And until then the company is in their hands."

"The board has absolute power," I mumble in disbelief. "We just have a seat like any other board member, one vote among many. No special considerations for being owners."

"Exactly." He slips the document from my trembling hands and turns it to the last page. The one that bears my name in my own curly handwriting.

And that just adds insult to injury—knowing that I, of my own free will, signed this fucking thing. I bound myself to these ridiculous, awful terms without even knowing what I was doing.

My stomach twists with the urge to be sick. Of all the legal documents that have ever passed through my hands, *this* is the one I sign without reading. Because I thought I knew what it meant. I trusted Dad and Prescott to give me all the information I needed. Hell, I trusted Dad and Bill Tate not to stipulate crazy shit in their wills in the first place. And I trusted Noah to bring any problems to my attention.

Blood thunders in my ears and I sway a little on my feet. "So that's what this is about? Trying to cement our control of the company?"

"I thought our inheritance was only contingent upon marriage at first. Then I saw the heir clause on our wedding day—well, our first one—and that's why I thought you ran off. But when you signed the contract, I figured you knew what you were doing. It took me about a week to realize you had no idea what you'd signed yourself up for. And then I just didn't know how to bring it up. Everything was going so well . . . with the company, and with us too. I didn't want to ruin it by saying something carelessly. I was waiting for the right words, the right moment."

I can't keep my mouth shut and listen to Noah defend himself any longer. I'm in no mood for excuses right now, and a million other more important questions are racing through my brain.

"But how . . . why? Why would our fathers do this?" My voice shakes with confusion, horror, and a fresh wave of outrage. I press my hands over my mouth again, as if that can stop my emotions from gushing out and splattering all over the snow-white carpet.

"Because they knew just as well as I do that we're meant to be together. And not in some fake marriage, some act that's all about publicity and business, but the real thing. A relationship that will stand the test of time."

*Are you shitting me?* I shake my head in disbelief. "I can't. You lied to me. Our fathers lied to me." I can still hardly wrap my head around the truth. Their betrayal—there's no other word for it—is just too staggering.

"Technically, they didn't. You just didn't read the . . ." Noah wisely trails off when I shoot him daggers with my eyes.

I suck in a deep breath and let it out slowly. All of a sudden, I feel like I'm deflating. Everything that makes me Olivia Cane is draining away.

"What should we do now?" Noah asks.

"How the hell would I know? I'm done." My voice is flat—too quiet, too steady.

He blinks at me owlishly. "What?"

"I said I'm *done*. I've had enough of all this shit. Close down the company, sell it off, do whatever you want. I don't give a fuck anymore."

This heir clause is one sacrifice too many. I've worked so hard and given up so much for Tate & Cane Enterprises. I let everything else in my life come second. I spent so many hard years in school and at my father's right hand. So many long days and late nights. I gave Tate & Cane my soul; I came close to giving Noah my heart. I can't give them my body too. Not to mention the next eighteen years of my life, until the kid grows up.

So my only option is just . . . leaving. Leaving Tate & Cane, leaving Dad, leaving Noah. I've had enough of men's control to last a lifetime. I'm sick of letting everyone except me dictate my destiny.

Noah's mouth drops open. "You can't . . . you don't really mean that."

"Don't you *dare* tell me what I mean. You don't get to make any more decisions on my behalf."

That kind of paternalistic bullshit is exactly why I'm

so pissed. Noah decided one thing after another about an issue that would totally change my life. He assumed how I'd react to the heir clause and decided that I couldn't be trusted with the truth, so he decided to keep me in the dark, and he almost decided me right into an unplanned, unwanted pregnancy.

And I had no fucking clue what was going on. I just went about my life, blissfully ignorant, thinking everything was fine, when all the while, Noah was hiding such a huge problem from me. Taking away my power to decide anything for myself. At best, he was a stupid, cowardly prick; at worst, he treated me like some kind of clueless pet, trapping me into a life I don't even know if I want.

Now he has the balls to stand here and look me in the eye and say a single solitary word about what's best for me.

Blinking back tears of rage, I whirl away from Noah and back to the bedroom. I start throwing clothes and toiletries into my suitcase, the same little maroon suitcase I brought to sleep over at our new penthouse. I still remember that first night. It wasn't so long ago, but it feels like a different life. I had been on the edge, unsure of how I felt about Dad's wedding gift, and Noah had calmed my nerves by welcoming me with sweet, hot kisses . . .

So stupid. I'm always so stupid. To think I was actually starting to hope. To get attached to Noah, to trust him, to think of myself as part of an *us*. I thought I'd learned something from the hell I went through with Brad, but I guess not.

Fate really is a cruel bitch. What are the odds of being so unlucky? I've only had two relationships in my whole life and both of them were disasters. Have I been wearing a big neon TAKE ADVANTAGE OF ME sign on my forehead or something?

This time, at least, I nipped things in the bud before any real damage was done. I may have wasted a couple of months on Noah, but that's a lot better than the two years Brad sucked out of my life. And it's not like I'm in love with the dickhead, right? At least I'll be able to cut him out of my life after a quickie divorce . . . or so I tell myself.

With my suitcase packed, I grab my purse and blow

past a shocked Noah, leaving behind the place I was just starting to call home.

# Chapter Two

*Noah*

I've spent the last two days sitting in my dark apartment, drinking until I can't feel anything anymore.

But it hasn't worked, because I still feel every emotion that was written on Olivia's face when she found me in the bathroom with the condom and the needle. Betrayal, disgust, the ultimate pain. I hated myself for inflicting pain on her like that. I swore I'd never hurt her. I meant every word of those vows I said to her that day on the beach. But now those words mean something even more.

Olivia isn't just my crush anymore, the girl I wanted to play house with. She's become my everything. She's the woman who's won me over against all odds . . .

And I'm just the douche who betrayed her.

"You realize what this means, right?" Sterling asks.

"What?" I snap. I'm not even sure why I invited him over. All he's done so far is annoy me.

Oh, that's right. I didn't invite him. After I'd gone AWOL from work for two days, he bullied his way inside the penthouse, saying he was staging an intervention.

"The only reason you're so upset over this is because you're in love with her."

I measure his words, turning them over in my mind. I don't want to even *think* the L-word. Not when she's gone and I have no idea if I stand a chance at getting her back. Instead, I just insist, "I'm not upset."

He chuckles. "No, you're right. You're destroyed. Heartbroken. Utterly devastated."

*Fuck.* I let out a heavy sigh, unable to argue.

"What the hell did you expect to happen?" he asks.

I shrug, fed up with his brand of tough love.

"Fine, then. You can give me the silent treatment all you want. But if you really love her, and I know you do, you know what you have to do, right?" When I don't respond, he says impatiently, "Go get your girl, you stupid bloody wanker."

If only it were that easy. I don't know where she went, and despite calling around, I haven't turned up any leads. She won't answer my calls. Fred is no use. And Camryn won't give me any information either.

"Believe me, I've tried."

"So you're giving up? Then you're in luck. This is nothing that a couple of strippers and a bottle of whiskey can't solve." Sterling grins.

Even though I know he's just trying to provoke me into action, I still make a sound of disgust. The old Noah would have handled everything in his life with debauchery, but lately, I have about as much interest in pussy that isn't Olivia's as I do in kissing Sterling.

"Not happening," I bark out.

"Come off it, mate." Sterling rolls his eyes and crosses one ankle over his knee, flashing me a bright paisley sock. "Noah fucking Tate went and got himself a wife. You wanted to pretend this wasn't going to change anything, wanted me to believe everything would continue as before."

"And your point?" My tolerance for his fancy British ass in my apartment lessens by the second.

"And the whole fucking world has changed, you included. You play to win, always have. As long as I've known you."

I nod, defeated. The bastard is right. I've always played for keeps when it came to Olivia. "So, what do I do now?"

"You're asking me? I already gave you my two cents." He leans his lanky six-foot-something frame against the back of my couch and smirks. "And I take it you've already done the ol' drag-the-beast-from-his-lair trick."

I scrub a hand over my face. *That's awkward.* I laugh, despite my foul mood. "God, I can't believe we actually used to do that."

"Hey, that trick won us the Murelli twins." His tone is the definition of authority on the subject.

"Still, don't you think it was a little fucking juvenile

that we used to pull out our cocks on a dare for girls to drool over?"

Sterling's boyish good looks and British accent, coupled with my charm and quick wit, used to gain us all the female company we could handle. But when we were feeling frisky and needed that extra push to close a deal, we were double trouble, whipping out the goods— each of us impressive in that department.

He smirks. "So you're telling me you never showed her your little buddy?"

"Don't be a dumb fuck. Of course I did." At the bar, on our *first date*. Super classy of me.

He laughs, the sound sharp and loud in the otherwise quiet apartment. "And she still left? Bloody hell, that's just depressing."

I pinch the bridge of my nose. He's like a fucking teenager sometimes. Never been in love. Never experienced anything like I had with Olivia.

"Her leaving had nothing to do with not being satisfied physically."

His smile fades.

"She left because I deceived her." I drop my head into my hands. "I should have just told her from the start."

Sterling claps a hand against my back. "Chin up. Olivia's a big girl; she should have read that contract. But yeah, you are kind of a cunt for not telling her."

Something I already knew. *Thanks for twisting the knife, buddy.*

"If we're done here, I'm going to go to the gym. I need to clear my head."

Sterling nods and rises to his feet. "We're done. Just call me if you need me."

"Will do."

Sterling heads out while I grab my gym bag and slip into my running shoes. I need to blow off some steam before I go insane.

Soon I'm at the gym, my feet pounding on the treadmill, sweat dripping down my back. Even if the workout is tough, I'm thankful not to be sitting within the four walls of our penthouse anymore. It's too quiet and empty. Olivia only packed an overnight bag when she left, and her rows of clothes and sexy high heels still rest next to mine in the master closet.

I crank up the speed on the machine and fight past the oxygen-starved pain in my lungs. My shallow breaths come too fast, but I don't care. I push harder. Faster.

Looking down at the clock on the machine, I see I've been at it for a mere six minutes. Seriously? Six fucking minutes? From the man who could easily run five miles through Central Park on the weekends?

Why does every minute without her in my life feel like an eternity?

Part of me doesn't want to admit it, but . . . maybe Sterling was on to something. What I'm feeling is heartbreak. Yes, my heart still beats, but it's broken. I never knew a love like I've felt for Olivia. And I've also learned that neither the company nor my career is worth losing her. All the money in the world means nothing if I don't have love in my life. My wife by my side.

And Sterling was one hundred percent right. I'm in love with her.

Slamming the heel of my hand against the red knob, I stop the belt and draw deep, cleansing breaths.

I know I can't outrun this problem. Being a man means facing it head on. I need to apologize to Olivia. *Again.* Make her listen this time.

Unfortunately, since she won't answer my calls, I'll need to fight dirty.

I shower and change in the men's locker room, solidifying my plan. Once I set it in motion, it will work quickly.

On the way home from the gym, I type out a text.

*NOAH: Snowflake, it's your dad. His health has taken a turn for the worse. Where are you?*

It takes only seconds for my phone to buzz in my hand. But rather than an answering text, she's calling me.

"Oh my God. What happened? Is he okay?" Her voice is panicked, and I hate that I have to do this. But I do. I need to see her. Need to win her back.

"I know you're pissed at me, but where are you? Let me come get you."

Olivia chokes on a sob. "I'm at David's place in the mountains. Hours from New York. Noah, please just tell me, is he okay?"

"He'll be okay. Text me the address and I'll plug it into the GPS. I'm on my way."

"Okay. Thank you."

I should be breathing a deep sigh of relief. Instead, I find jealousy clouding my judgment. "Just one more thing . . . who the fuck is David?"

Rather than answering, she lets out an exasperated huff and hangs up the phone. *Well, then.*

My phone chimes with the address and I head off, with nothing to do with three hours except stew over who the fuck this guy is that she ran off to for comfort.

After an hour on the road, I can't take it anymore. I call Camryn.

"Who the hell is David?" I snap once she answers.

"Hello to you too, grouch," Camryn says with a huff.

"Tell me, Camryn."

She lets out a long sigh and I hear the TV switch off in the background. "So you got her to crack, huh?"

"I'm on my way to pick her up at some guy's house. I deserve to know what the hell is going on."

She barks out a humorless laugh. "Rrrright. Just like Olivia deserved to know you were plotting the entire time to knock her up."

I guess the cat's out of the bag. But what did I expect? I went to my best friend for advice; it only makes sense that Olivia did too. I take a deep breath.

"I wasn't plotting, goddammit. I was torn up over the whole thing. It became obvious that Olivia never read the contract, and I was trying to figure out the right thing to do."

"In what world is 'the right thing' sabotaging a rubber so you get her pregnant?"

"I love Olivia and wanted to make a life with her. A baby would have eventually been in the cards, right?" A little chubby thing with her blue eyes and a gummy smile. The thought makes me grin.

"Except that you never even asked what Olivia wanted. You just assumed. And were going to bully your way into her uterus come hell or high water."

I grit my teeth. "It wasn't like that." *Except, fuck, it was. I'm the world's biggest asshole.*

"You're in deep shit, Noah. Not even your magical nine-inch strawberry-flavored dick is going to save you this time."

"Yeah," I mumble. "Got it."

"Good luck."

I end the call and double-check the directions. Camryn was no help, but it doesn't matter. I'll be there soon enough, and I *will* get my woman back.

I hit the gas pedal and zip off down the road, that

much closer to whatever the future holds.

• • •

When I pull into the circular driveway in front of a freaking mansion built into the side of a mountain, I do a double-take to make sure I have the right address. Sure as shit, whoever this David is, he lives in a fucking ski resort, by the looks of it. And based on the lack of cars in the drive, I'm wondering if he and Olivia have the place all to themselves . . . and how they've been keeping busy.

Climbing the front steps, I brace myself for what I might find inside. But before I can knock, the large glass door swings open and Olivia's standing at the threshold with a pissed-off glare in her eyes.

"I can't believe you," she barks and then storms away.

I follow her inside, taking note of the cozy cabin-chic decor and the gourmet kitchen with a rustic barnwood table for ten. "Olivia, I—"

She stops in front of a massive stone fireplace that rises to the beamed vaulted ceiling. "Using my father's health as a bargaining chip," she scoffs. "Is nothing off-limits with you?" Her posture is stiff, but I can see her hands trembling.

"I'm sorry about that."

She rolls her eyes. "I called him the second we hung up. He was at home resting, said he was totally fine." Her gaze drops for a second. "Well, not *fine*. But nothing's changed."

I step closer to take her shaking hands in mine. "When shit hits the fan, you run. It's what you do. It's what you did when we were first presented with the contract. Then again at our wedding when Brad blackmailed you. And now, when I fucked up. Real couples don't run from their problems. We have to work on this together, and that means talking it out."

She yanks her hands away. "Great, I'm all ears. I can't wait to hear how you're going to talk your way out of this one."

I hear footsteps behind us, and watch Olivia's expression turn neutral as her eyes track who I assume must be David. Fighting off a smirk, I turn around.

David looks to be our age, with shaggy brown hair and a pleasant grin on his face. "Hey. Sorry to interrupt." He turns up his palms. "I'm David. Noah, I assume?"

"The one and only. Did you enjoy my *wife?*"

His grin vanishes as his eyes narrow. "I don't know what you're implying, but Olivia is an old friend from college. When she called needing a place to crash away from the city for a few days, I opened my door to her."

Olivia's hand on my shoulder stops me. "Don't be a dick, Noah. I don't know if I'm even going to be your wife after this."

My gut twists and I swallow down a lump in my throat. "Fine. But it's time to go." I have zero interest in hanging around with her pal in his mansion.

She crosses the room, without the argument I expected, and gives David a hug and a kiss on the cheek. They speak in hushed tones, and after he gives her a final hug, she heads for the front door, ignoring me completely.

I follow behind her, giving David a curt nod.

I'm afraid it's going to be a long, silent drive back to the city.

And for the first fifteen minutes, it is. We speed down the highway, the only sound the quiet hum of the air-conditioning. Miles tick past and Olivia sits motionless beside me, staring straight ahead at the taillights of the car in front of us, making a point of neither looking at me nor avoiding me. The subtle scent of her vanilla honeysuckle perfume teases me from the passenger seat.

I'm still pissed off, still unsure how to proceed. There's no manual for how to be a good husband, and I've fucked up plenty. But my heart is in the right place. Still, it hurts more than I thought possible that she ran off to some other guy for comfort.

"Did you fuck him?" I finally blurt, cutting through the silence.

She tenses. "What?" Then she turns toward the passenger window, not letting me see her face. "Don't be an idiot."

"Did. You. Fuck. Him," I repeat, my hands

tightening on the wheel.

"You have no right to that information." Under her breath, she adds, "Just as you had no right to my uterus."

"Fucking hell I do."

Her head suddenly whips around. "What if I did? Would that piss you off? What if I said that he licked my pussy and fucked me until I screamed his name?"

My foot jams the brake. I haul the car over to the side of the two-lane highway. I slam my fists against the steering wheel and inhale angry breaths, my nostrils flaring.

"Goddammit, Olivia."

"Let me get this straight. You're mad at *me*?" She scoffs aloud, crossing her arms over her chest. "You have some fucking nerve, you know that?"

"You ran to another man for comfort, Snowflake. How am I supposed to feel? I'm your husband."

A bitter laugh that sounds more like a yelp bursts from her lips. "Some husband. Do I need to remind you of all the various ways you've fucked up within the past forty-eight hours?"

I hold up one hand. "Please don't. I'm miserable, Snowflake. You can't possibly know how sorry I am."

Something flashes in her eyes and for just a second I see . . . sympathy? But then it's gone, replaced by her steely reserve. And that's the precise moment I know I'm fucked. It's one thing to imagine how she was feeling, but it's quite another to see the hurt still burning in her eyes, to hear the venom in her voice. This isn't going to be easy.

"Were you really going to do it? Get me pregnant without including me in the decision?"

I swallow and loosen my grip on the wheel. "I'm not going to lie to you. The thought crossed my mind. But then I knew I couldn't. Wouldn't be able to live with myself if I did something like that."

"And when I caught you in the bathroom?"

"It was a moment of confusion. Weakness. Desperation. I promise you, I wouldn't have gone through with it."

She nods once, then looks down at her hands. "Just take me home."

"I have somewhere better in mind."

• • •

When I roll to a stop in front of the Cane family estate outside the city, Olivia unbuckles her seat belt and climbs from the car without a word. I called Fred on my way here and asked him and Prescott for a quick meeting.

Fred's standing in the foyer. As we approach, he shifts nervously.

"Hi, Dad," Olivia says, giving him a brief hug. She might be pissed off at him too, but he's a sick old man, and her father. Something tells me her forgiveness will come a lot quicker for him than for me.

Fred tips his head toward the study. "Go have a seat. Prescott and I will be right there."

As we head toward his office, I swallow the last of my pride because I know this conversation is going to be a difficult one. I've taken advantage of Fred's trust in me—tricked his little girl. I feel about two inches tall.

We take our seats at opposing ends of the mahogany table and settle in to wait.

Olivia's gaze cuts over to mine. "Why in the world were you fucking me with condoms if you were supposed to get me pregnant?" she hisses.

"Because it was what you wanted." My voice is soft and Olivia's eyes are wary, like she wants to understand my true motivations. I hate this part of our relationship. I hate that I lied to her, and that I don't know how to fix it. "You asked to begin a physical relationship. Of course I wanted that too, but you were in the driver's seat. I tried to give you what you wanted. And as far as getting you pregnant without your consent, I never could have gone through with it."

Her mouth turns down into a frown. Now she doesn't look angry so much as confused. She stares at the platinum wedding band on her left hand, turning it over and over while we wait.

# Chapter Three

*Olivia*

Prescott arrives about ten minutes later and takes the seat next to Dad. We're evenly spaced around the conference table, as if nobody wants to get too close to anyone else.

I used to play in Dad's study as a child, under this very table. Its familiar mahogany surface is smooth and cool beneath my clammy palms. With every slight move of my hand, my wedding band ticks against the polished hardwood like a clock. Counting up or counting down, I'm not sure. I'm even less sure about why I haven't taken off that damn ring and thrown it in the Hudson River.

With us four the only attendees, the atmosphere should be relaxed; we're family, after all, with the exception of Prescott. But it's even stiffer and stuffier than a typical business meeting. I can't quite look any of these men in the eye—especially Noah. Every time I try, my emotions start roiling again, threatening to spill over, churning so ferociously that I can't even tell what I'm feeling. I shouldn't have sat across from him, but the alternative would be going near him.

The way Noah finagled a chance to talk to me today, when I'd already made it clear I didn't want to talk, I still can't believe he had the balls to do that. I was already ultra-pissed at him for hiding the truth about the heir clause. Telling me that Dad was on death's door was just piling lies upon lies. Did he really think that *more* deceit would help his case?

I saw right through his plan, of course, but that doesn't matter. What matters is how deep Noah seems determined to dig himself. (Although I couldn't help but be a little insulted by the obviousness of his lie. How stupid does he think I am? I called my father the second we hung up.)

And then to top it all off, he started interrogating me the instant he set foot in David's place, accusing me of letting all sorts of strange penises into my vagina. What the fuck? He acted like I was the one who'd done something wrong and needed to account for my behavior. Even if I *had* screwed David, my sex life wasn't Noah's business anymore. He forfeited all husbandly rights the instant he chose to conceal my own inevitable pregnancy from me.

He didn't even tell me anything when he barged in. He just kept insisting that he'd never do anything to my body without my consent—totally contradicting the scene I stumbled into that night—and bitching about how much his regrets hurt. I could tell that he was genuinely sorry about damaging my trust, but that didn't mean my trust wasn't still damaged. I wasn't going to forgive his stupid, selfish decisions just because they backfired on him. The asshole made his bed, and now he can lie in it . . . far, far away from me.

Although, speaking of bed, one thing he said did give me pause. When I asked him why we were using condoms if he was trying to knock me up, I was struck by the plain way he said, "Because that's what you wanted." As if the reason was obvious. As if my wishes, my desires, were his first priority. I'm still not sure what to make of that, in the context of everything else that's happened lately.

And somehow, despite all my anger and hurt and

suspicion, I found myself agreeing to come back for an emergency meeting with him and Dad and Prescott. Temporarily, mind you, just to try putting this mess behind me . . . but still. How does that man always persuade me? How does one look into his intense dark eyes always end with me believing in him?

Maybe I was just sick of always running away from disasters. Noah had hit a nerve with that comment. One way or another, I wanted closure. A definite end to this story, leaving no room for regrets or second guesses later on down the road. Closure.

Whatever my reason was, I got in Noah's car. I let him drag me down from that Catskills retreat and back to civilization. And two hours of driving later, I'm sitting here in the house I grew up in—where I have no choice but to stare our problem in the face.

I do my best to push down my feelings and find the cool, rational mindset I work best in. Now isn't the time to wallow in negative emotions. I can't let my confusion and anger and sadness run away with me . . . yet again. Noah arranged this meeting to get everything out in the open and everyone on the same page. If all goes well, we might even be able to start straightening out this mess. I can wait until I'm back in my own private space to scream or cry or tear my hair out, or whatever the hell my wounded heart desires.

Except I don't have my own space anymore. Shit, I almost forgot. What are we going to do about *that* little issue? Unless I want to kick Noah out of the penthouse, or rent a hotel room for the foreseeable future, I'll have to see him every night. I'll have to deal with his puppy-dog eyes following me around the room, silently begging me to understand his side of the story and accept his apology. I'll have to see his handsome face, feel the warmth of his toned body, when I don't know if I'll ever be ready to let him touch me again. We'll have to keep living together in our marital home . . . when I'm feeling anything but wifely.

Dad interrupts my dour thoughts by getting the ball rolling. "Noah filled me in on the phone about what's happened the past couple days," he begins.

Oh, great. Even though this is what we've come here to discuss, I hope Noah didn't provide *too* much detail. Tight-lipped, I nod at Dad to continue. "And your thoughts are?"

His bushy, graying eyebrows fly up. "I'm appalled, of course! I'm so sorry things ended up like this. Neither Bill nor I ever meant to deceive you."

"Then how did this happen?" I ask. "Why was this weird pregnancy stuff even in his will in the first place? How did it end up in the inheritance contract?"

Dad clasps his hands tightly together where they rest on the table, and gazes at me with an earnest, almost pleading look. "We added the heir clause into our wills on a whim. We both wanted grandchildren . . . it was our fondest wish to see you two kids together, and the family you'd build for yourselves one day. We figured you'd fight us on that point and we'd just cross out the whole thing. It was wishful thinking."

"But Bill Tate died sooner than anyone expected," Prescott explains, "so the heir clause slipped into his will unseen and unchallenged. And after that point, it had to be included in the inheritance contract."

"Jesus, this thing got passed around like a bad penny," Noah murmurs.

I make a point of ignoring him. "But surely we could have done *something*. Asked a judge if he could rule that clause unenforceable and declare a partial revocation . . ." Or at least find some loophole or tricky way of fulfilling it that didn't involve me actually getting pregnant.

"Yes, we could have looked for other options," Prescott says. "I would have worked with you to find an alternative solution if either of you had objected."

Dad leans forward. "But when you didn't, I was a little surprised but I figured you must be okay with it since you'd signed the contract."

That was Noah's argument too. I groan internally at the reminder that I signed without reading every last word.

"And I thought, heck, maybe they'll have fun trying to get pregnant. It would keep both your minds off the failing company." Dad sighs heavily, the lines of age and fatigue and regret etched deep into his face. "I'm so sorry, sweetheart. I meant this inheritance to bring you together and make you happy, not tear you apart and make you miserable. I feel terrible, like Bill and I both failed our children."

I swallow around the sudden lump in my throat. "But how did you know? How were you so certain that pairing us off like this was the right thing to do?"

"Because it's always been obvious that you two were meant for each other. You've been in love all along. Ever since you first met, when you were three years old and he was five." Dad's expression lifts into a slight, fond smile. "And your mothers agreed. All four of us knew our children . . . we could read the signs."

"Mom? She thought this was a good idea too?" I blurt.

"If I remember correctly, she might have even been the one to suggest it."

Stunned, I blink. All along I assumed that this arranged marriage was only concocted by our fathers. Are our entire families just fucking nuts? Or . . . were they on to something? Four people, two of whom ran a multibillion-dollar international company, couldn't all be wrong . . .

Prescott looks almost as uncomfortable as I feel.

He probably didn't come here prepared to be drop-kicked into the middle of an emotional battleground.

"Even as toddlers, you two were inseparable," Dad continues. "Literally, on some occasions. You fought like cats and dogs, yet somehow ended up laughing and playing happily five minutes later. You always wanted to sit together whenever we sat down for a meal or a movie or anything like that. And if we tried to move you . . ." Dad chuckles. "Oh, the tantrums we'd get! When we went to the water park for your fourth birthday, Olivia, Bill tried to take Noah to the men's room and you both nearly had a conniption. Your mothers had to take you together to the women's and you held hands under the wall between stalls."

What? How have I never heard this story before?

And more importantly, how is this relevant?

"That was over twenty years ago," I protest. "I hardly see what it has to do with us now."

From the pinched expression on Prescott's face, he agrees with me. Neither of us expected a trip down memory lane.

But once Dad gets started rambling, he can't be stopped. "Oh, but I've got dozens of great stories about you two. The first time our families vacationed at the beach together—all the summers before then, you were still too young to travel far from home—Noah accidentally sat on your sand castle and you started crying, so he built you a new one and found a starfish to decorate it."

"I think I actually remember that," Noah muses. "And you gave me your ice cream when I dropped mine."

"Here's one you might have been old enough to remember. Olivia, on your first day of elementary school, some boy was hassling you on the playground, and Noah punched him right in the kisser. Bought himself a one-way ticket straight to the principal's office. And he marched the whole way there with a smile on his face, happy to take whatever punishment he was given. For you."

Now that Dad mentions it, I do remember this story. I guess some things never change. That exact same scenario—Noah rushing to my defense—has played out with Brad not once, but twice recently. And he'd do just about anything for Rosita too. Noah still has the same strong sense of justice, the same streak of protective compassion.

He just cares *so much* about people. And he approaches life from his gut, not his head. That hot-blooded quality is something that I've come to appreciate, as a fresh perspective in the workplace, charm in an unconventional romance, and a sexy rush in bed. It's not that I don't care about people; it's just easier for me to set aside my emotions in order to think clearly, whereas Noah feels so fiercely that he can never escape their pull.

From the way he talked about our duty to Tate & Cane, it was clear that the thought of laying off our employees ate him up inside. Bad enough, I guess, to paralyze him, to bar him from telling me the truth until desperation broke him free.

But that doesn't change anything. Doesn't erase his lies or heal my wounded trust. His general depth of feeling or capacity for caring isn't the issue on the table here. If he really cared about *me* specifically, he wouldn't have hidden the truth for so long and then scared the hell out of me that night. He could be the best man in the world to run this company and still be the wrong man for me.

"Don't forget what happened the next day," Noah says, unaware of my racing thoughts. "That same kid made fun of me for getting in trouble—when he got off scot-free, the little shit—so Olivia kicked him in the giblets and went to the principal's office too."

Dad bursts out laughing. "Really? I never heard that one. I guess Susie kept a few secrets from me after all." He inclines his head at me. "But that only proves my point. At the first hint of someone messing with him, you came running, ready to teach them a lesson."

How weird. I must have cooled down with age . . . because the only other explanation is that I'm more similar to Noah than I thought.

"That's hardly the only time she's saved me." Noah turns his affectionate smile to me, his dark eyes crinkling at the corners, and I just can't look away. "I'd wait until the last minute to start school projects, then panic and beg you for help, and you'd roll your eyes and scold me, but you always gave me advice and checked my work. I don't even know how many times—"

"I can give you an estimate," I remark dryly. "It was about fifteen, maybe twenty."

"I admit, I had my head up my ass until after I graduated from high school," Noah says with a sigh.

"Only until then? That's not how it seemed to me."

Noah turns up his palms with a shrug. "Okay, fine, after college. But who doesn't?"

Dad interjects, "You had your silly moments too, sweetheart. When Noah first started dating—you were twelve, I think—you were so irritable for months. Out of nowhere, you would start ranting about how 'I don't care about that stupid jerk, he can do whatever he wants' when no one in the room had suggested otherwise. Or even brought up the subject at all, for that matter."

My cheeks flame red as Noah starts laughing. "D-dad . . ." I squawk.

"Oh my God, that's perfect." Noah chuckles. "I

can just picture it. It's exactly what you would do."

I glare at him, still blushing. "Shut up."

"But he made up for it," Dad says. "For your fifteenth birthday, he gave you a framed picture of the first hundred digits of pi, written in binary."

Now it's Noah's turn to go a little pink. "Jesus, that was so dumb. I just figured, hey, she likes numbers and math and stuff, right?"

I shake my head. "No, I loved it. It's still hanging in my room upstairs."

He blinks. "Really? You kept that stupid present? I'm surprised you even remember it."

"It wasn't stupid. And of course I remember." Realizing how mushy that sounds, I hurriedly add, "That was the night you totaled your first car on our way to the country club, and I offered to walk with you so you wouldn't feel weird. But then we ended up waiting for a bus because I didn't realize how hard it would be to walk five miles in high heels. I was an hour and a half late for my own birthday party."

"But do you regret spending that time?" Noah asks, his eyebrows raised playfully.

"I sure as hell regret trying to dance the tango with you afterward. My feet hurt just thinking about it."

Although I also remember the breezy, full-moon summer night, Noah smiling at me, my friends being jealous that I'd made a dramatic entrance with such a handsome senior who didn't even go to our school . . .

"Speaking of gifts," Dad says, "what about the time when you were in third grade and Noah gave you a set of diamond-and-platinum earrings? You didn't even have pierced ears yet. And then it turned out that Noah had 'borrowed' them from his mother's jewelry box."

Prescott clears his throat impatiently. "Not to interrupt, but could we get back to discussing the contract?"

Wait, he's right. What the hell am I doing? We're here to talk about the heir clause and how to salvage our inheritance. How did I get sucked into family-story hour? I'm reminiscing about my past relationship with Noah when what matters is our company's future.

I shake my head as if I can dislodge all this silly nostalgia. "I agree with Prescott. Why are we talking about this stuff? We're not here to sing 'Kumbaya' and share cute anecdotes. We're here to clean up a serious mess . . . a mess that *you* had a lot to do with, in case you forgot."

And with that, the slowly lightening mood plunges back into grave silence.

"I wouldn't have phrased my objection in quite those words," Prescott says after an awkward second, trying to be delicate.

"You asked how Bill and I knew you two were meant for each other," Dad says gently.

Abruptly I stand up, pushing out my chair with a squeak of wheels. I can't do this right now. I wanted to, but I just fucking can't. My brain won't work with Dad and Noah looking at me. I have to get out of here if I want any hope of sorting out my own feelings and figuring out what I want to do next . . . assuming I can even do anything at all.

I tamp down my instinct to apologize for making

the atmosphere tense, for cutting our meeting short, for everything. I'm not the one who screwed up here—Noah is.

Instead, I just mutter, "Excuse me. I have a lot to think about."

And with that, I turn and leave Dad's study, my head buzzing so loudly I can't hear whether anyone calls after me.

# Chapter Four

*Noah*

"Can you pass me the orange juice?"

Those are the first words Olivia's spoken to me in days. Ever since the confrontation in her father's study, she's been as cold and icy as ever. Not that I can blame her. I did try to conquer and pillage her uterus like it was my own private jungle gym.

"Here you go." I hand her the carton across the counter. She's seated at the breakfast bar with her laptop and bagel while I'm at the stove frying an egg.

It's our first weekend back home together since everything went down, and I still have no idea where we stand or what to do to win her back.

Instead of brainstorming about how to right this mess, the meeting with her father turned into a sweet reminiscing session, which Olivia promptly shut down.

"The gala's tonight," I comment, sliding the lone

egg onto a plate. Weeks ago when we RSVP'd, it was assumed that we were attending the charity banquet together—with Olivia as my plus one, my partner in crime. Sure, it was a work event, but there'd be dinner, champagne, and dancing. It was a date, for all intents and purposes.

"Yup," is all she says, her eyes still on her laptop screen.

"Okay. I have a car coming at seven."

"I'll be ready," she says coolly.

She'll play the part well—doting wife, professional CEO, happy banquet-goer. Her mask will be firmly in place tonight. My goal will be to break through the facade.

"See you then."

I grab my keys from the counter and head out. No way I'm sticking around in her deafening silence today. I've said my apologies, groveled to her, even included her father in the conversation, and she's still holding on to anger.

That's her choice. From this point onward, we'll either work this out and make it as a couple—or not. The ball's in her court.

• • •

"So this is how one of Manhattan's best attorneys lives? Nice place." I stand in the center of Sterling's newly renovated studio apartment in the heart of Manhattan, appraising the recent remodel.

"It should be for what I paid, but thank you."

Sterling purchased the top floor of a historic building that was undergoing renovations more than six months ago. By the time he finished gutting the entire thing, it boasted a modern kitchen, brand-new bathroom, sleek polished wood floors, and cool neutral colors on the walls. It's decorated well with pieces of art and stacks of coffee-table books and even some patterned throw pillows on the slate-gray sofa, but it's not feminine. Just well put together, like it's had a woman's touch. It makes me miss home.

"We're not staying here. Come on." Sterling grabs his wallet and cell phone and heads to the door.

"Where to?"

"We're going out. To where I should have taken you in the first place."

Soon we're at our favorite gentleman's club, seated along the bar with a view of the stage, two pints of beer in front of us.

"Now this is somewhere to drown your sorrows," Sterling remarks coolly.

My gaze drifts over to the center stage, where a petite blonde makes the stripper pole her bitch. But I think my cock must be broken, because despite the show she's putting on, there's not even the slightest bit of interest. Nada. Nothing. I look down at my lap. Urging my cock to do something. Waiting to see if it moves, if it twitches, anything to make me see that it's not broken. She couldn't have broken my cock when she broke my heart, could she?

Sterling leans forward on his elbows to give me a pointed look. "You want to know my grand unified theory of life?"

"I have a feeling you're going to give it to me

anyway, so sure." I flash him a tight, fake grin and take another sip of my beer.

"Why get yourself all spun up over one woman, one *difficult* woman, when there are so many flavors to sample?"

He turns, gazing over at the action on the stage. All shapes and sizes of naked women shake their goods for us to enjoy. This is the biggest gentleman's club in the city, and the choices are endless. From lean runner types with pert breasts and firm butts without dimples, to curvy goddesses whose huge breasts sway when they walk. From redheads that you instinctively know are trouble, to platinum blondes who are probably wild in bed, to demure brunettes who are every man's perfect girl-next-door fantasy. But none of them appeal to me. Like, at all.

"Not interested," I choke out, my throat feeling tight. What the hell has happened to me? I was Noah fucking Tate—master of my own domain, professional charmer and booty-call provocateur.

"Come fucking on," Sterling says on a groan. "Not a one?"

I shake my head. "Nope." None of these women hold a candle to the classy, sophisticated woman who used to warm my bed at night and keeps me on my toes all day. She makes me work for every inch of ground I gain with her. The feeling is addicting. Any of these woman would happily go home with me if I asked. Where's the fun in that?

Sterling makes a low, tortured growl of frustration. "You're impossible."

I cut my gaze over to his. "Right, because your life is so perfect and full. If it was, you wouldn't be at a place like this."

I know I'm on to something. Sterling doesn't open up much, but from what he has shared, I know his job makes him miserable much of the time, and living here while his entire family is still back in Great Britain is hard.

But he holds up his hands, taking no offense. "I was only trying to help. Chill."

There is no helping me. There's only an unmet need raging through my body and soul. I need to get

Olivia back. I need to be inside her. To claim her. To make her see that she is my wife. Till death do us part.

I take another sip of my beer, knowing I'll get my chance tonight.

# Chapter Five

*Olivia*

The charity gala is beautiful. The finest, most mouthwatering cuisine is laid out on long tables along one wall of the opulent banquet hall. A tailcoated band plays lively smooth jazz on the stage set up at the other end.

Throughout the rest of the huge room, hundreds of upper-crust guests mingle and laugh and dance. White-shirted waiters slip fluidly through the crowd with silver trays of hors d'oeuvres and champagne flutes. The high bay windows stand open, letting a crisp breeze ruffle my chiffon evening gown and play over my bared shoulders and back.

And I can't enjoy any of it, because the heir clause is still hanging over my head, casting a dark shadow over everything.

Even just a week ago, I would have been proud to stroll in here on Noah's arm. And unfortunately he does look devastatingly handsome in his tuxedo. But after what he did, I don't want him near me. I don't want to pretend to be the lovey-dovey young couple, all picture-perfect smiles. Because I can't simply erase what I saw from my brain.

That one tiny moment in the bathroom threw our whole relationship into question. It's almost like we're back to square one. Before I got to know him, before I saw him as anything more than an annoying, lazy playboy. Before I (*almost*) fell in love. I have to decide all over again whether I can trust him.

And even if I do trust him . . . what then? Let him put a baby in me? Sacrifice my body, my future, in exchange for a company that might end up drowning no matter what we do? I won't be forced into having a child. If and when I have a baby, it will be because I'm ready to parent. And I'm a long way from believing that the person beside me in those fantasies is Noah.

My grim thoughts derail when Noah rests his arm around my waist, his hand on my opposite hip. I stiffen at his touch. The line between his brows deepens; he definitely noticed my flinch.

"Christ, Snowflake, try to loosen up," he mutters under his breath.

"I'm still angry with you," I say out of the corner of my mouth, still smiling brightly. The strain of keeping up our happy facade is already taking its toll on my nerves.

Noah's expression darkens despite his trying to repress his frown. "Be angry all you want, just don't act like it. We have to make this look good. The last thing the company needs is the media starting rumors that our relationship is on the rocks."

"I know that, I just—"

Noah cuts me off. "Don't look now, it's the CEO of Acentix Telecom." He inclines his head toward a silver-haired gentleman walking our way. "Act natural. Touch my arm or something."

"I'll pass," I hiss just as the man claps Noah on the shoulder.

"Noah Tate, you son of a gun." He laughs, louder than necessary—the room isn't *that* noisy. "How've you been lately? Is this lovely creature your wife?"

Noah's gaze flicks toward me, too fast for anyone else to see. I know what he's thinking: *For now, anyway.* But he responds smoothly, "I'm proud to say she is. Olivia, have you met Caleb Tyrell?"

I nod at Mr. Tyrell. "Yes, at all of our client meetings with Acentix." *And yet this idiot still managed to forget me.*

"Ah yes, of course. How could I forget such a pretty face?" Caleb winks at me.

Normally I would play along with his corny old-fart flirting. But I have no patience left for putting up with men tonight. I just nod and smile, more stiffly than before.

"Sweetheart, your hand is empty. Let's go get you a glass of prosecco." Noah steers me away from Mr. Tyrell under the pretext of us going to the bar.

I set my jaw. Why did he have to jump in like that? Intervening so obviously only makes the situation more awkward than it already is.

Fortunately, Mr. Tyrell doesn't seem to notice anything wrong. "As much as I'd love to shoot the breeze, I should get back to my own wife before she gets jealous." With another obnoxious wink in my direction, he ambles away and disappears into the crowd.

"What the hell is your problem tonight?" Noah growls under his breath as soon as the client is out of earshot.

"You just have to be in control of everything, don't you?" I snap right back. I could have handled myself smoothly in that situation, if he'd only given me a chance. Just because I needed his help with Brad doesn't mean Noah has to be my white knight all the time.

"Okay, that's it. If you want to fight, let's at least take this somewhere private. Then you can make as big a scene as you fucking want."

I match his dark glare. "Great idea."

Noah stalks through the banquet hall's entrance. I follow him as he turns down a seemingly random narrow hallway. Even from behind, he looks almost as pissed as I feel—his shoulders are tense and his stride is even longer than usual, forcing me to hurry after him.

Gradually the buzz of chatter from the banquet hall fades, leaving only the clack of our shoes on the marble floors. When we reach a coat closet, he yanks the door open. "After you." He follows me inside and shuts the door behind us, plunging us into shadows.

I launch into my tirade as if there had been no interruption. "What the fuck do you *think* my problem is? I can manage faking a happy relationship for the press, but don't expect me to enjoy it."

I can just barely make out Noah shaking his head. "We both know that's not the whole story. You've been freezing me out for days now. If you've got something to say, say it. I'm listening."

What is it with men and not understanding basic communication? "I've already made my feelings very clear. You just don't like the messages you got."

"Oh, come on." He sighs. "Throw me a bone here. I know I fucked up royally, and I'm sorry, but things between us have been going nowhere lately. Can I at least get a hint about where I stand? Am I going to stay in the doghouse forever? Just let me know what I should do, how I can fix this."

"It's not that easy. Do you think you can just buy me some flowers and I'll forget all about what I saw that night? The heir clause will disappear out of the contract, we'll inherit the company, and live happily ever after?"

"You said you were giving up. Quitting the company, or quitting our marriage, or maybe both—I couldn't exactly ask for clarification while you were tearing ass out the door. But then why are you still here?" Noah's silhouette throws its hands up. "If you hate me so much, why haven't we gotten a divorce yet? Are you giving this another chance or not? I'll stay by your side, or I'll leave if there's really no hope left, but I won't hang around just to be your punching bag."

I swallow past the knot in my throat, fighting the urge to cry from sheer anxiety and frustration. "I don't know, okay? Even if I believed everything you said— about how you'd never get me pregnant without my consent—what's next? What are we going to do? No baby means no inheritance."

"*If* you believed me?" He releases an exasperated scoffing sound. "You don't even know that for sure? Wow, I guess I really am on your shit list."

I doubt he can see me roll my eyes, but I do it anyway. "Gee, I wonder why. There's no reason on earth why a woman should distrust a man who lied his ass off about things that could make or break her whole future."

"I said I was sorry. I made a big fucking stupid mistake, okay? I didn't speak up when I should have, because I was so scared of losing you and ruining the company and—"

"The company is going to be ruined anyway!" I explain for what feels like the hundredth time. "If you had said something earlier, we could have figured this out together. Instead you waited until the last possible second."

"Is saving Tate & Cane the real reason why you're so tense? Because I'm here to help with that."

"Please don't tell me you're hitting on me," I reply in my driest, coldest tone.

"No, that's not where I was going." His voice drops slightly, taking on a silky note. "Although if you want me to . . ." He leans against the wall, trapping me between his arms.

I turn my face away from his. Having him this close makes it hard to think. "Ugh. No thanks."

"Fair enough. All I meant is that we're partners—we can think of a way out of this problem, if you'll just let me help you."

Why hasn't he backed off yet? His spicy cologne is slowly filling my head with fog. "I think I have the right to be a little skeptical of a man who I caught with a fucking needle."

Noah makes a quiet growling huff. "See what I mean? You bring that up again, and I already apologized and explained what happened. We're just going in circles." His voice smooths out again into an imploring, seductive tone. "Please, Snowflake. Don't shut me out. I'll do anything. Just tell me. Say the word and I'll be on my knees—begging forgiveness, at your service, ready and willing to make it up to you."

His warm breath fans ticklishly over my cheek as he speaks. That voice is pure sin, licking at my self-control like flames.

I try to retort, "Y-you're ready and willing for that anytime. With just about any woman too."

"You know that's not true. Maybe I was that way once, but now ... I'm a one-woman man. You've caught me for good. I'll never be satisfied with anyone but you ever again."

And suddenly, his hands clasp my bare shoulders and his lips press hot against mine.

I gasp into his mouth. My eyes slide shut helplessly. I didn't realize how much I needed this contact, this closeness, until Noah's touch lit my nerves on fire. But now I'm painfully aware of every minute it's been since he last made love to me.

I'm still pissed at him. Damn his sexy smirk, damn his wickedly skilled kiss, more intoxicating than anything I've drunk tonight ... I don't want to want him. But I do want *this*. Dear God, I might even need it.

And so I let myself give in.

It's okay as long as he doesn't talk. As long as he doesn't remind me that we're Noah Tate and Olivia Cane, heirs to a failing company, with the board's impending decision hanging over our heads like a guillotine blade.

Right now, under cover of darkness, we're anonymous. Just a man and a woman, a pair of animals who are starving for each other. I can pretend that this is only sex, only blowing off some steam, and it's not because I'm still addicted to Noah despite everything that's happened between us. I can come back to my senses—to my waking life, my anger and hurt and worry, all the crushing responsibilities of my family name—after my body is satisfied.

At the exploring swipe of Noah's tongue, I open up and return his kiss savagely. He gives a little surprised noise, then a growl of satisfaction. His lips curve against mine in a smug smile.

Does he think he's won me over? Then he'd better fucking think again, because I'm going to make him fight for every inch of ground. I crush my mouth against his, and when he gently nips my lower lip, I answer with a harsh bite. He moans and matches my intensity right back. Soon our kiss is little more than a dance of dueling tongues and soft murmurs of pleasure.

Still devouring my mouth, he leans into me, walking me backward until my lower back hits a shelf. I jolt at the brush of cold metal on bare skin. Then he pushes a little more for good measure, forcing me to arch my spine and raise my chin, exposing my neck. The shelf's chill soaks through the thin fabric of my dress and spreads goosebumps over my arms. But I'm already so hot, I barely notice any of it. My senses are too completely consumed by Noah's touch and taste and smell.

He hikes up my evening gown's skirt and gropes me, his fingertips tracing up my bare thighs until I can't stand it. I know exactly where his destination is, and I want him there now.

Lifting the elastic edge of my panties, his fingers glide over my center in one easy stroke. "No matter what, Snowflake, you're always wet for me." His voice is rough with need, but his movements are controlled.

"Sh-shut up and do something about it," I gasp.

"As you wish."

He gently pets my clit, my blood racing, heart

pounding as I rock my hips forward. It's too slow. Torturous.

Finally, need wins out over pride, and I beg. "More."

"I hope you're ready." And with that, Noah's control snaps. He yanks down my damp panties and shoves three fingers inside me.

My head almost hits the wall as it falls back. I dig my nails into his shoulders, urging him *harder, harder*. He plunges his fingers in and out with rough jerks of his arm. It's still not quite enough; I want his cock, long and thick. But I'm not so far gone as to forget that we're in public. So I make do.

And in a way, this rough fingering is better than fucking. It's all for me, all about my pleasure. I can feel his steely erection against my inner thigh, twitching with eagerness, but he doesn't get jack shit until I decide he deserves it. I reach under his moving arm and grab his crotch through his pants, just to feel how hard he is and to hear him groan in frustrated need.

And he does. The sound is harsh and needy. It

makes my pussy grip his fingers hard, quivering as his desperate growl washes through me.

His hand is a surprisingly decent substitute for his cock. Every thrust rubs the ball of his thumb against my clit and strikes the spot inside me that shoots hot lightning through my veins, making my toes curl in my Manolo Blahniks. All the bare hangers on the shelves around us rattle with his force.

"Faster, dammit," I grunt out between thrusts. He's pounding the breath out of me in sharp, guttural bursts—stifled growls reminding us both that I'm still angry as hell.

"You asked for it." His arm pistons faster and I bite my lower lip hard enough to bruise.

He suddenly breaks our kiss, leaving me with nothing to stifle my whimpers, and his mouth descends to suck and bite at my neck. I want to tell him that he's a dead man if he leaves a hickey, but I can't form words anymore. All I can do is cling to him, clawing at his shoulders. I arch my hips up and spread my knees to urge him even deeper inside me. He fucks me as hard as he can into the wall while I hang on for dear life, gasping and trembling as the pleasure rises higher.

My thighs clamp around his forearm as I finally tip over the edge. No longer able to thrust with his arm's full strength, Noah crooks his fingers to massage my G-spot and grinds the heel of his hand into my clit. I shudder violently, my mouth opening in a silent scream, wave after wave of white heat pulsing through my entire body. Noah keeps working his hand to let me ride out my climax to the end.

Floating slowly down from my high, I can feel myself still spasming around his fingers, my inner walls gripping tight and relaxing and then gripping again, weaker and weaker each time. I flush deep red at the thought of just how much Noah can feel. He could tell the moment I started to come and the moment my orgasm finally faded away. There's nothing I can hide from him when I'm like this.

His fingers slide free with a faint slick noise. His eyes are dark with lust as he brings his fingers to his mouth and sucks them clean. My knees tremble a little. God, he's infuriatingly sexy.

He steps closer to loop an arm around my bare

back and he kisses me, tenderly now. I can taste myself on his lips. I'm feeling so languorous that I relax into his embrace without thinking. His cock is still rock hard in my hand. Instinctively, I reach out to unzip his pants and reciprocate the pleasure he just gave me. Even through his tuxedo, his body is so warm against the breeze trickling down from the ceiling vents, the chill I somehow never noticed before . . .

It suddenly seeps into my spine and I shiver, blinking like I've just woken up from a dream. *Wait . . . what am I doing? Why did we just . . . ?* My jaw tightens. The fog of lust is clearing fast and goddammit, I've made a huge mistake. I'm supposed to still be pissed at him, but yet again, I let my libido take the reins. How does this always happen?

I yank my hands off Noah's crotch like I've been burned. Giving in to pleasure was bad enough, but giving in to the desire to please him . . . I'm acting like we're making love. And as much as I try to tell myself it was just force of habit, I know it wasn't. I wanted to get him off almost as badly as I wanted to come myself.

"What's wrong?"

Noah's voice is still husky, so ready for my touch, and I shake my head like I can dislodge the seductive sound.

"You already know."

My cheeks burn with embarrassment as I hike my panties back up and smooth my skirt. I let him get so far. He still has so much sexual power over me. He can play my body like a violin, and the rest of me is helpless to follow.

"Hey, where are you going? What about me?"

Ignoring Noah's protests, I charge out of the closet like something is chasing me. As if I can outrun my own feelings. I fling open the door . . . just in time to lock eyes with Mr. Tyrell, walking down the hall. His eyes widen in confusion.

"Got lost looking for the bathroom," I blurt, and stomp back to the main room as fast as my high heels will let me.

# Chapter Six

*Noah*

If Olivia is going to stay mad, fine. So be it. But if last night is any indication, we still have chemistry. With my fingers buried deep inside her, she came apart, clawing at my suit jacket, devouring my mouth, gasping for air. She can pretend to be unaffected all she wants, but I know the truth.

And she's still here, sharing our apartment. She hasn't filed for divorce or started looking for a new place or anything like that. So I have to believe that, deep down, she does still have feelings for me. Her father was right—growing up, we were so in sync, right there for each other through every rite of passage. Granted, I'm sleeping on the couch, but at least she hasn't left.

I'll just have to find a way to make her *believe* those feelings, show her that we belong together. Convince her that the happily-ever-after she's always wanted isn't just a fantasy—it's something we can have together, for real. But it's become obvious that I'll have to fight dirty. And that's why I've enlisted the help of our friends. *This is gonna take a village.*

"Where's Olivia today?" Camryn asks, surveying our empty apartment as she enters.

"At the spa." I usher her over toward the dining room where I have everything set up. I booked Olivia for the works today—European facial, hot stone massage, manicure, pedicure, and something called a blow-out, which I'm told is for her hair. "We have at least four hours," I add.

Olivia thinks the appointment is just my latest attempt to apologize for everything, but really, it's because I needed her out of the house so I could hold this brainstorming session.

Camryn nods. "I'll help however I can."

I appraise her as though I'm looking at her for the first time. Her mischievous green eyes have a sparkle to them and her expression is open and curious. "Why the change in attitude?" I ask. She once told me she wasn't *Team Noah*, after all.

Camryn helps herself to one of the bar stools at the breakfast bar. "Because." She flips her long chestnut-colored hair over one shoulder. "I've seen how good you guys can be together. In just a couple short months, you were the cause of so many positive changes in her. She worked less, she laughed more. She wasn't just all about the grind."

I nod, hanging on her every word.

"She had pleasure in her life too—something that put a smile on her face, and that something was *you*."

A smug grin uncurls on my mouth. "I couldn't agree more."

"But." She purses her lips like she's tasted a lemon. "You did fuck up royally."

My grin fades to nothing. "I did."

"Epically. Like, completely fucked up beyond anything that's normal."

*Okay, Jesus, I get it.* I interrupt her before she can rub any more salt in the wound. "And that's why I've invited you guys here today. We'll start as soon as

Sterling gets here."

The buzzer sounds, signaling his arrival.

"Speak of the devil," I mutter and head to the intercom to buzz him in.

Sterling grins and claps his hand on my shoulder when he arrives. "Ready to get your girl back?"

"Hell yes."

My posture relaxes, and I lead him into the dining room. Having the support of my best friend means the world to me, and gives me the tiniest bit of hope that maybe this is possible. Sterling's always been the voice of reason, after all. If he believes in me, maybe I really can pull this off.

I gesture for Sterling to take a seat. He does, next to Camryn at the counter. They watch me with wary expressions. I stand next to the easel with the new flip charts and markers I purchased just for the occasion. The dining table is scattered with poster board, sticky notes, and extra markers. I only hope we'll be able to figure out a workable plan today. Never in my life have I wanted something as badly as I want to fix my relationship with Olivia. To bring us back to the happy place we used to be.

Growing up, I always envied what my parents had. Sure, I've spent years playing the field and indulging in meaningless conquests, but I've always known deep down that I was a one-woman kind of guy and I'd eventually want to settle down. To attain that kind of comfortable familiarity that comes with monogamy and commitment. And now, just when I've gotten a taste of how good that can be—it's been savagely ripped away from me by my own stupid actions.

I clear my throat. "First, thank you both for being here today. It means a lot."

Sterling nods for me to go on. Camryn looks a little skeptical but stays quiet, waiting for me to continue.

"As Camryn pointed out earlier, yes, I have fucked up royally. And I don't intend to make any excuses for my behavior. I only want to tell you that I was a desperate man, at the end of my rope. And that I love Olivia . . . and probably always have."

Camryn's expression softens and she leans back in

her seat, placing her hands in her lap.

"I've brought you both here today to help me create a strategy for winning back my wife."

I repeat the words I practiced in the shower this morning, pausing to write OPERATION: GET OLIVIA BACK on the flip-chart paper taped to the easel.

I hear Camryn snicker and look over at my captive audience. Sterling is gazing at me, his mouth open like I've lost my damn mind.

"What?" I ask, feeling defensive. I've barely begun, and they're giggling at me behind their hands like children.

"Olivia has rubbed off on you." Camryn chuckles. "The old Noah would have winged it."

I consider her words for a moment. Just as I open my mouth to ask if that's such a terrible thing, Sterling interrupts.

"And the old Noah would have had pizza and beer."

At that, Camryn perks up. "Oh, pizza sounds great.

I haven't had lunch yet."

I fish my cell phone from my pocket and toss it to Sterling. "Fine, order pizza. And there's beer in the fridge. But we're going to work through this, and you're going to help me figure it out."

Camryn salutes me while Sterling presses the phone to his ear to order two large pies.

It's been five minutes and my strategy meeting is already fucking derailed.

• • •

Paper plates with pizza crusts litter the coffee table, along with a few half-empty bottles of beer. The poster board I bought has turned into a mess of scribbles, after Sterling challenged Camryn to a game of hangman and then tic-tac-toe.

The easel holds a large drawing of a penis, which Camryn assured me with a sober expression was the key to getting Olivia back. Right now, they're laughing and adding words like *vulva* and *scrotum* to the mess.

I want to slap both of them.

All their suggestions were silly and unhelpful. This entire afternoon has been a huge waste of time, and now I only have an hour before Olivia's due to arrive home.

"Okay. That's enough." I grab the Sharpies from their hands. "If you're not going to take this seriously, then get out. Both of you."

Camryn rises to her feet and yawns. "Sounds fine to me. I'm going home . . . I need a nap."

Sterling pats me on the back—in sympathy or to mock my efforts today, I'm not sure. "You'll think of something, buddy. I know it."

"Thanks," I reply, unconvinced.

I usher them out the door, then systematically make my way through the apartment, wadding up the used papers and collecting the markers. I stuff the remnants of our lunch into the trash and then collapse on our bed, grabbing her pillow and holding on to it, her scent all around me. I stare blankly up at the ceiling.

I glance at the clock. I now have forty minutes before I can expect Olivia home, and I still have no idea what I'm going to say to her when she gets here. How the hell am I going to convince her about us? It's been days and I haven't come up with jack shit.

Rising to my feet again, I begin pacing the room. When I see the black lacquered box that sits atop my dresser, I stop and go to it. Cradling the box in my hands, I sit back down on the bed. I don't often take trips down memory lane; just keeping the mementos safe in my home is usually enough. But today, I need some guidance.

I take each item out, holding it and inspecting it before setting it down one by one on the bed beside me. One of my mother's lockets. A leather bookmark from her favorite dog-eared romance. The token my father received from the New York Stock Exchange the day his company went public. A water-stained coaster from the seafood restaurant where he proposed to Mum. A friendship bracelet Olivia gave me in the sixth grade, its braided thread fraying and dull. I smile and set it aside as I look through the rest of the treasures I saw fit to save.

After inspecting all the various small tokens that

hold meaning in my life, I come to the last thing, buried in the bottom of the box. The folded square of newspaper that contains my mother's obituary.

Just the feel of the soft, worn paper in my hands makes the hair on the back of my neck stand up. *What would she think of me?*

I'm forced to take deep stock of my life. It's unraveled to the point that I can barely recognize it. *Where did I go wrong?* I put trivial things that don't matter before love. If the company goes down . . . so what? We have to look for new jobs? *Big fucking deal.*

Of course, I don't want to lose the company and watch my friends and employees struggle to piece their lives back together. But as far as my own life goes, my marriage is so much more important than the company name printed on my paycheck. To save those jobs, to save myself from loss of face, I put everything above my wife. If Olivia grants me a second chance, I won't do that again.

I unfold the newspaper, delicate with age, and gaze upon the words I've read many times before:

*Dahlia Emerson Tate was taken from this world too soon. Having moved to the United States as a teenager, she later attended Smith College and then married William Tate of Briar Grove, New York. She is survived by her husband and a bright, caring, and inquisitive son, Noah. She firmly believed that her son was her biggest achievement, and raising him was her greatest pleasure in life.*

Mum sure as hell knew the importance of love and family. She would probably be so disappointed in me right now.

The lump in my throat grows, and I force a deep breath into my lungs. I haven't cried over my mother's passing in many years, but something about her loss feels fresher than ever. Maybe it's because I've destroyed the only good thing in my life, and I don't have her here to dole out advice, or pat my head, or hug me close.

"I'm sorry, Mum," I murmur. "I'll fix this somehow. I will make you proud. I promise."

# Chapter Seven

*Olivia*

I check in at the spa to discover that Noah has booked me for the works. I'm being treated to a European facial, a French mani/pedi, a hot stone massage, and finally a blow-out. I'm briefly annoyed that Noah booked my appointment under "Mrs. Tate" instead of "Miss Cane." But I shrug it off. Whatever . . . it's a free spa day, and after everything that's happened in the past week, I badly need some downtime. If this is his way of groveling, I'll take it.

But I'm so tense that I don't even begin to relax until the massage, over an hour into my appointment. Even while I'm lying on my front, my eyes closed, the tiny blond masseuse rubbing my sore, knotted muscles, my mind can't help wandering back to the same dismal ground I've been mentally pacing for days now.

All along, I was operating under the assumption that once we got married, Noah and I would have ownership on our side. Those extra rights and responsibilities would both force the board to listen to us and make them more willing to take risks, since we'd assume more of the burden in case their gamble went sideways. But the fucking heir clause means that inheriting Tate & Cane isn't an option anymore.

Is that really the end of the world, though? Is there still another way out?

In a matter of weeks, the board members will meet to cast their votes and decide our company's fate. But the question isn't settled yet. They still have a choice to make—either retain Tate & Cane or sell it off. And they'll approach that choice like businessmen.

It all comes down to which option will make them more money. How much value we're likely to create in the future compared to how much they can convince another company to buy us for. Long-term versus short-term profit. Risk and reward.

Even as things stand now, it's not like the company is a terrible bet. It's performed pretty well under its new management; our profits have definitely started climbing toward the black over the past couple months. But our gradual turnaround hasn't quite been the jaw-dropping comeback that would banish the board's doubts. We're still more of a gamble than they would like.

If we can't use our ownership privileges for extra clout . . . well, that definitely still handicaps us, but our defeat isn't assured yet. We'll just have to make ourselves indispensable in other ways. We need to demonstrate two things: Tate & Cane is worth more alive than dead. And it's worth more with Noah and me at the helm than with anyone else they can dig up.

Okay, so we show them some new numbers. Some flashy, sexy predictions they haven't seen before. But based on what? We can't just pull a bunch of graphs out of our ass. I know enough finance to massage the statistics a bit, but there's got to be something to massage in the first place. Optimistic projections are one thing; bald-faced lies are quite another. Even if we can fool the board in the short term, we'll just be left holding the bag later, and begging for another chance won't go nearly so well the second time around.

Releasing a heavy sigh, I try to loosen my stiff shoulders so the masseuse can do her job. It's damn near impossible to relax with all this on my mind.

There's no way around it—we need solid evidence to back up our fairy-dust forecast. We need an assload of new clients, or at least some promising prospects, and we need them ASAP. But already we've been hustling like crazy for months. We've tried everything. We've tapped everyone. At this point, we'd just be pestering the same people and annoying the hell out of them in the process. How pathetic would that be? Nobody enjoys a hard sell. And I don't even know if I have the energy for that anymore.

Unless . . . we can encourage them to come to us, instead of us chasing them. Can we create a scenario where corporate bigwigs actually *want* to hear our pitches? Or at least something to make them receptive, relaxed, willing to listen, willing to take a chance on new deals.

*A fun, laid-back atmosphere . . .*

Free food and drinks are always a guaranteed hit, even with billionaires who can damn well afford their own. Ideally, in the interest of time, we would gather as many prospects in one room as possible so we can woo them all at once instead of scheduling a zillion individual meetings over the course of several weeks.

But we'd need it to be more than that, it would have to be the best damn party this city's ever seen.

Inspiration strikes like lightning. I bolt up from the massage table with a gasp.

"Mrs. Tate? Is something wrong?" the masseuse asks, startled.

"No, it's okay." Something is very right, in fact. I can't stop myself from grinning with excitement; she probably thinks I've gone crazy. "Sorry to be so abrupt, but I have to leave. Please go ahead and charge me for the full hour."

Without waiting for her response, I dash behind the curtain and throw on my clothes while texting Noah.

OLIVIA: *Meet me in my office. I have a plan.*

And if my instincts are on the mark, it'll turn this

company around for good.

• • •

After dark like this, especially on a Sunday night, the building is deserted. I've been here before at odd hours, and such deep stillness always gives me an eerie feeling, like I'm the only person left on the planet. But I'm on a mission now, so I hardly notice. The silence gives way before the quick, steady tapping of my footsteps as I walk to my office.

By the time I hear Noah coming down the hall, I've already typed out a press release and fired it off to the *New York Times*. *Boom!* I pump my fist in the air, feeling giddy with the surprise attack I'm about to unleash on the business world.

Noah steps inside my office without knocking. "What the hell is going on? You said you had an idea?" He doesn't need to add, *It better be a fucking fantastic one to drag me into work on a Sunday evening.* He must have dropped everything to hurry straight here—he's wearing jeans and an old T-shirt, his hair disheveled.

"I do. I've already sent out a press release." I take a

deep breath to ease the fluttering in my stomach. "Picture it—we're going to throw the biggest, best gala New York City has ever seen. We'll invite all the corporate bigwigs from firms we've wanted to woo, but didn't know how to snag meetings with. We'll show a brief presentation at the start—no more than ten minutes—just a few bold, hard-hitting, buzz-worthy clips of our company in action, the results we've achieved for our clients . . ." I wave my hand. "And then we mingle."

Noah is still standing in the doorway, squinting at me like he can't quite parse my words. "So you're saying . . . we're going to throw a party?" he asks skeptically. "This is the grand plan I put on pants and hauled ass halfway across the city for?" His tone is serious, but his smirk tells me he's not actually mad. I've found there's very little he wouldn't do for me.

I nod eagerly. "Exactly. It'll solve everything."

"You're going to have to convince me."

Unable to sit still any longer, I jump up and start pacing the narrow space between the wall and my desk. "How many times have you been to a conference or whatever, and by the end, you've seen so many presentations you can't even remember who was promoting what, because they were all abstract and boring and nearly identical? If we want people to remember us, we have to be memorable. Which means being fresh and different—and being *fun*. This party will make Tate & Cane stand out in their minds and will create a psychological association between us and all sorts of positive feelings."

Noah sits down in the chair in front of my desk, as if he's a client I'm pitching to—which I guess he kind of is. "I get what you're saying, but it still seems all very fuzzy and touchy-feely. It's hardly a guaranteed solution."

"I know this party idea isn't money in the bank, but I'm not just spitballing here, either. Storytelling is a well-proven branding strategy."

"For content marketing, yeah, but—"

"When clients contract with us, they're not just purchasing our services—they're buying into the idea of *us* as people, on a personal level. Our charisma or our character or whatever. It's not necessarily wise or rational, but it's human nature. We're social, emotional creatures . . . we value relationships and narratives and 'gut feelings' very highly, even when we don't consciously know we're doing it."

And I learned the importance of this idea from Noah himself. I almost have to laugh when the irony of my words hits me. We've had so many arguments about business just like this, but on opposite sides of the table. If only briefly, I've turned into Noah, the optimistic, intuitive social butterfly, and he's turned into me, the practical, analytical worrywart.

"Instead of just drowning people in dry numbers," I say, "which is hard to pay attention to and even harder to remember, we give Tate & Cane a face they can identify with. We show off our business by showing off ourselves. The two new young CEOs who are ready to think outside the box and push boundaries. People eat up that kind of story with a spoon!"

As I grin at Noah, his own lips start to quirk up. "Okay, okay . . . maybe you're on to something here."

I cross my arms and cock my head, pretending to be insulted. "Just *maybe*? Please, do try to curb your enthusiasm."

He chuckles. "Fine, Snowflake, it's a fucking fantastic idea. When did you tell the press this party was going to be?"

"Next Saturday night."

"That soon? Damn, we've got our work cut out for us." But Noah is still smiling. Evidently my excitement is contagious. "I guess we should get started." He rubs his hands together and gives me the broad grin I've been waiting for since he arrived.

"Right now?" I assumed he'd want to get back to whatever he was doing at home.

"What better time?" He pauses to look at his watch. "Actually, let's get some dinner first."

My stomach growls in agreement and we both laugh. I forgot that I haven't eaten since breakfast, before I left for the spa. Speaking of which . . .

"Thank you for the spa package. It was perfect. Really, thank you."

He nods. "Glad you enjoyed it."

We debate between ordering pizza or Chinese, call the latter, and break into our delivery boxes at the long oak table in one of the conference rooms. As we wolf down our egg rolls and chow mein noodles, Noah asks, "Does your dad still keep a bottle of Scotch in his desk drawer for clients?"

I swallow my mouthful of rice. "Yeah. Why?" At Noah's smirk, I shake my head. "Oh, hell no. We're not getting drunk . . ." But then I stop. Because, really, why not? I'm in a celebratory mood, and one drink with dinner won't kill me.

"Come on, one drink. Two tops," Noah says with an airy wave of his hand. "We'll buy him a replacement bottle. He probably won't even notice anything different."

"We're breaking into Dad's liquor stash like a couple of teenagers."

"Yeah, isn't it nostalgic? I don't think we've done that since I was . . . a junior?"

I chuckle even as I roll my eyes. "Sure, let's have a toast. I think we've earned it."

"Hell yes, that's the spirit." Noah gets up. "I'll be right back."

A few minutes later, he returns with a squat crystal bottle of honey-colored whiskey, about half full, and two tumblers.

"Sorry there's no ice," he says as he pours our drinks. "We'll just have to take them neat, I guess."

I'm not much of a hard-liquor drinker, but I shrug. "Whatever. I'm sure I'll survive."

I scoot my brimming glass closer, bend low to the table to take a sip—then immediately start coughing. Oh God, I spoke too soon about the "surviving" part. It's like inhaling fresh hot smoke, with the way it burns on the way down. *Ugh . . . people drink this stuff willingly?*

Noah laughs at me and I give him the evil eye, but soon I'm giggling too.

He tastes his own and gives a little lip-smacking sigh of satisfaction. "Damn, that's good."

"How can you drink that?" I say with a grimace.

"It's an acquired taste . . . just like you." He dodges

my playful swat.

As we polish off our Chinese dinner, we toss around party plans including theme, catering, decorations, and guests. One shot of Scotch somehow becomes two, then three. Turns out it goes down easier the more you have.

Even though we both still don't know where we stand with each other, the mood is jubilant. My flash of inspiration, and the optimism it brings, is too strong to be undercut by any relationship awkwardness. I'm even more drunk on hope than I am on Dad's whiskey.

I stand up to throw away my empty takeout box and the room sways a little. Okay, maybe hope and whiskey are about equal by now.

"Whoa, there," Noah says, rising to his feet. He reaches out to steady me with a hand on my hip.

I turn . . . and find myself far closer than I expected. If I took even one step forward, I would be in his arms. The mood changes from one of business to a sultry encounter between two old lovers swamped by sexual attraction and history.

"You okay?" His voice is low and smooth, just as intoxicating as the liquor.

"Y-yeah," I reply, suddenly even more light-headed. "You?"

Why did I say that last thing? I must be a lot more drunk than I thought. But Noah answers with a serious tone and only a slight smile, as if my question made perfect sense.

"I'm feeling pretty good right now." He pauses, then adds, "But I could be better."

Somehow, without noticing, I've leaned closer. Or was I always this close, and just never noticed the tickle of his breath on my lips? I inhale his familiar spicy scent and feel my knees weaken again.

"H-how do you mean?" I ask.

"That depends on you," he replies. Then he hesitates again. He traces his thumb over my lower lip. "It's nice to see you smiling. I . . . missed you."

Closer again. The atmosphere in the conference room, once happy and uncomplicated, holds its breath as we gaze at each other. Noah's dark eyes are solemn. But if I look deep into them, I can see something smoldering. For me.

I can't tell who moves first, me or him. Closing the distance feels as natural and inevitable as falling. All I know is that his lips feel warm and soft and so good, so right against mine. I open up and hear him sigh as our tongues tangle together.

"Missed you," I hear him murmur again against my mouth. "So much, Snowflake."

Our kiss soon deepens, urgent and wild. The heat of his hands all over me—my breasts, my ass, my thighs, seemingly everywhere at once—burns right through the fabric of my clothes. I'm softening like taffy, melting and melding into him. I suddenly realize that the longer I avoided this, the more explosive it was bound to be when we rekindled.

The back of my legs hit the conference table. I lose my balance and sit down with an ungraceful thump. Without breaking our kiss, Noah slides between my parted knees, pushing my cotton skirt up to press his whole body against me hungrily, as if he can't get enough contact. We fit together perfectly, chest to chest, the hard length of his cock insistent on my belly. When he lifts my legs to haul me even closer, my calves wrap around his angular hips automatically, even before my squeak of surprise escapes my lips.

His mouth descends again, coaxing my lips to part as he strokes his tongue so skillfully against mine. His warm palms massage my breasts and I reach down between us, flicking open the button on his jeans. And then he's in my hands, and I take pleasure in each stroke, every labored breath, every moan I draw from this big, sexy man—evidence that he's mine and mine alone. Nobody else can make him react like this. His cock is warm, steely, and I massage every inch of it, delicately rubbing the hot drop of fluid that's leaked out over the tip.

"Snowflake, I . . ." Noah's voice is tight with need. But he doesn't have to ask, doesn't have to say anything else. I need this too.

I wriggle back, just far enough away to snag my purse with one hand and drag it over the table to me. I take out the foil packet hidden in my wallet. His eyes widen at the sight. But neither of us speaks; the silence is deafening as I tear open the condom.

He pushes his jeans and boxers the rest of the way down his hips. I roll the condom over his cock. We barely dare to look at each other. This moment floats as light and as fragile as a soap bubble; the touch of reality would burst it instantly. One careless comment, one reminder of our unpleasant situation, and we'll come crashing back down to earth.

But it's obvious that we're both thinking about the condom. Such a small thing, so heavy with significance now. A minefield of uncomfortable, unresolved questions still stretches between us, my own emotions reflected in Noah's hesitant expression. What does this mean in the long run? Are we okay again? Am *I* okay? Or will tonight be the last time we ever touch?

I can't bear to answer those questions yet. I just want Noah. I don't want to think about why I want him, or whether I trust him, or what the future holds. In this moment, I know he's my everything.

I pull aside the dampened crotch of my silk panties. Unprompted, he guides himself into me, pausing when I hiss through my teeth, and slowly pushes forward when I roll my hips in impatience. Inch by hot, thick inch, he fills me, taking away the empty space between us. And then his mouth descends on mine, our kiss hungrier and fierier than ever before.

Words are too heavy and too light, too sharp and too blunt, all at the same time. The low, breathy sounds of pleasure are all the communication we need, anyway. So I push all other unpleasant thoughts away and enjoy this, enjoy *him*. The sensation of skin on skin dissolves the past and future, leaving only the present. My whole world shrinks down to the sensation of his thick length parting me, of hot breath and hotter friction.

"Noah." I gasp when he reaches between us to rub my exposed clit in gentle circles.

"I know." He grunts, still buried to the hilt. "So perfect. Me and you."

And he's right. It is.

I flex my inner muscles around him and he groans.

Our gasps and moans wordlessly guide us toward bliss as we writhe together. Soon Noah is slamming into me, giving me every hard inch of himself, the soft sounds of wet flesh slapping so erotic and forbidden in the dim, silent office.

My toes curl and I clench around his girth with every thrust. I abandon everything and let myself fall into him—Noah Tate, my husband, my rival, my betrayer, my partner. This walking contradiction, the one man I can't seem to stay away from, who makes my emotions simultaneously so confusing and so clear.

Tomorrow morning, I should come back to this hot, tender memory and try to figure out what it means. Maybe I will. Or maybe I'll tell myself it was all a dream.

For now, though, I don't ask questions. I just feel.

# Chapter Eight

## Noah

Watching Olivia work the room is incredible. Everything we've worked so hard for over the last few months has led us to this very moment.

"Hanging in there?" she asks, stealing a moment away from the crowd trying to garner her attention. Lifting onto her tiptoes in her already sky-high heels, she presses a quick peck to my cheek.

Ever since our erotic encounter in the conference room last weekend, things have been good. Not *great*, but *good*. She's been polite and chatty at home, and while we haven't totally made up—or had sex again, for that matter—things have felt okay. Like we're moving in a positive direction, even if it's only by an inch at a time.

It's safe to say that the party Olivia dreamed up is a smashing success. Tate & Cane has delivered—*big fucking time*. We're winning over everyone from the tired old CEOs to the young, hungry marketing execs ready for the next big thing. I'm practically beaming with pride for my gorgeous wife. I'm trying to keep my optimism cautious, but damn, it's impossible not to get caught up in the moment.

"This is amazing, baby." Giving her waist a squeeze, I return her chaste kiss on the cheek. I won't cross the line and show her too much affection, because I know this isn't the time or place and it would only make her uncomfortable, but I can't resist taking a moment to let her know how much her sweet gesture means. We've worked hard to get here, and while I'm still not sure what the future holds for us, this is a huge step in the right direction.

The look in her eyes is tender, and there's a small smile on her lips. "I'll check in with you again later."

For the most part, we've divided and conquered. I've hardly spoken three words to her all evening, but I've kept her in my line of vision, and she's never been far from my thoughts. I watch her blend back into the crowd. With her simple black slacks and emerald-green silk blouse, she looks stunning. Professional, but more casual than usual, which fits the mood perfectly.

This is no boring business meeting, nor is it the politically correct, awkward, boring "work outing" that everyone silently dreads. We have fucking Beyoncé performing. Okay, so she's not Beyoncé, but the girl is gorgeous and fiery and she can sing her ass off. The atmosphere is casual and chill. And the waiters aren't serving chilled champagne, they're serving cucumber cocktails strong enough to put a smile on the lips of even the stuffiest company leaders.

Hell, most everyone else is in bare feet on the sod floor we had brought in. Beach balls are being kicked around. Hammocks where Fortune 500 leaders lounge with a cocktail. These people don't ever get time off, so Olivia's ingenious idea tapped into the one thing that they truly needed—to chill.

Maybe I really have rubbed off on her. A smile pulls on my lips.

I head toward the buffet line, scoping out who else I might talk with tonight.

The food isn't pretentious. It's accessible and reminiscent of childhood. Simple finger foods. S'mores over a fire pit. The smell of grilled hot dogs in the air.

It's friendly and easy. And since I haven't eaten since lunch, I stop in line next to a gray-haired man I recognize as the chairman of a major tech firm.

When I meet his eyes, his gaze skitters away, and a look I recognize flashes across his features. The guy is overworked, tired, and probably has another four or five hours of crap to do tonight once he gets home. He just wants to be left alone. The last thing he wants to do is talk shop. Which is fine by me. I remember my own dad sitting at the dining table with his laptop long after Mum and I went to bed at night.

"Hi, I'm Noah." I offer him my hand and he shakes it. No last name, no title, because I can read his hesitation like it's a flashing neon sign.

"I'm Howard Dillon of Spherion, but before you begin . . ."

"Have you ever had a walking taco?" I ask him, grinning like I know the world's best secret. Because I do.

His mouth closes, then opens, then he shakes his head. "As a matter of fact, I haven't," he says finally.

My smile grows wider. "Dude, let me hook you up."

Howard chuckles and follows me up to the front of the buffet line.

And soon, we're seated cross-legged on a blow-up couch overlooking a water balloon fight, bonding over corn chips and seasoned ground beef.

Howard kicks off his shoes and wiggles his toes encased in black silk socks. "So this is a walking taco, eh?"

I help myself to another bite and nod. "Strangely good, isn't it?" It's all the standard taco ingredients mixed into an individual-sized bag of corn chips, which can be eaten with a fork. I had a roommate in college who once introduced me to the idea.

"You guys at Tate & Cane seem to have it all figured out." He takes another bite. We haven't even talked business, but I already know I have him right where I want him.

"We work hard, we play hard, and most of all, we get it. You're a busy man with a lot on your plate. If we can make your job a little bit easier, that's what we're here for."

He makes a sound that sounds a lot like approval.

My gaze swings over to find Olivia again and she gives me a quick thumbs-up. She's bounced from table to table, doing her best to show each guest the same level of personalized treatment and respect. She approaches every conversation like it's the only one that matters, like the person in front of her is the most important, interesting thing in the world. It's a major talent, that's for sure.

I don't have to tally tonight's numbers to know we've been more than successful at winning over new clients and striking new deals with existing clients. And best of all, it's been easy, casual, and fun. I'm in awe. My wife is one amazing creature.

Later, I throw Howard's trash away along with mine, and get us each a fresh beer. "Thanks for being here tonight."

He rises to his feet. "Hey, no problem." His right hand disappears into his pocket, and a second later he hands me his business card. "Here's my direct cell. Let's talk late next week when I'm back from China. I'd love to see what we could do with some fresh talent helping us."

I nod. "I'd like that." My pocket is full of business cards and promises for follow-up meetings. I can't recall the last time business has been so good.

Toward the end of the evening, I'm itching to send everyone off with their parting gifts—goodie bags filled with fine French chocolates and a gift card for a massage on us—and get Olivia alone. But there are still at least a dozen people here, along with a couple of corporate bigwigs jumping in a bouncy house.

I chuckle and head over to sit with Olivia. She's abandoned her heels and is perched on a bar stool deep in conversation with Estelle from Parrish Footwear, the woman who, when we were first dating, Olivia thought I was flirting with at a business dinner. It's good to see them getting along like old friends. Laughing and smiling as they talk.

Just before I reach them, Olivia rises from her stool, excusing herself to take a phone call. I'm not sure what could be so important that she'd cut a client meeting short, so I watch her from the corner of my eye. Her brow furrows and she paces back and forth as she listens to the caller on the other end.

*If this is Bradford fucking Daniels again, so help me God . . .*

"Babe?" I place my hand on her wrist.

"I'll be right there. Thanks." She hangs up and swallows hard.

"Snowflake?"

"It's my dad." Her voice cracks ever so slightly. But that small loss of control tells me everything. If she can't keep her cool in public, in front of so many guests . . . whatever she just heard must be devastating.

I know that she'd never be able to live with herself if she broke down within earshot of our guests. With my hand on her lower back, I quickly usher her from the banquet room and out the front doors.

Once we're outside, she inhales a huge breath and tears spill from her eyes.

"What is it?"

"His nurse called. He's being rushed to the ER. He fell and hit his head."

*Shit.* Ever since Fred's final treatment failed a few weeks ago, his health has been getting progressively worse. So much so that he rarely comes into the office anymore, and he hired a nurse to watch over him at home.

"You need to go," I say. "Go to the hospital and be with him."

"Are you sure? What about . . ." Her gaze drifts back to the party, where we can still hear the band playing and the guests' happy chatter.

I grip her shoulders and lean in to press a kiss to her lips. "I've got this. We're wrapping up anyway."

She nods and wipes away the tears that keep escaping despite her bravery.

"Do you want me to come with you?" I offer.

She shakes her head. "No. Make sure you see everyone out and follow up on every deal."

A smile crosses my lips. "Of course I will. I'll see you at home later?"

"Yes, I think so."

We share a small, meaningful kiss, and then she's gone.

# Chapter Nine

*Olivia*

Two weeks and what feels like fifty gallons of coffee later, Noah and I have closed all the deals we started at our big beach bash.

It seems like half of New York City is still buzzing about that party. Our company's financial future is about as secure as it's going to get—we've got a dozen fat new contracts and three times as many promising network contacts to tap into for years to come. Tate & Cane Enterprises is doing amazing. I should be on top of the world . . .

Except this morning, I woke up to a voice mail from the hospital. Dad's health has taken a sudden turn for the worse.

Two weeks ago, on the evening of the big networking gala, Dad was apparently working late in his study—which he shouldn't have been doing, damn it, but I've never been able to keep him away from his job.

He fell down in the hallway somehow, probably on the way to the bathroom. He either stumbled or just plain passed out. His night nurse found him lying unconscious and called 911.

That night, it was all I could do to keep from bursting into terrified, angry tears as I drove at top speed toward the hospital. Every horrible thing that might have happened to Dad flashed through my brain in a gruesome slide show. God only knew how long he was lying there on the carpet. He could have died right then.

Screw the party—I should have been there. I should have checked in on him more often. Hell, I should have found a way to keep his stubborn ass in bed in the first place. If I'd just tried harder, looked after him more closely, been a better daughter . . .

A blaring honk jerks my attention back to the road. I try to concentrate on getting to the hospital again without adding another family casualty to the mix. Those self-blaming thoughts were unproductive two weeks ago, and brooding over them now is no better. But they still gnaw at the back of my mind.

After what feels like hours but is probably only twenty minutes, I reach the hospital. I park in the rear lot, shove a handful of quarters into the meter, and rush inside. I check in with the front desk nurse, but I don't need her to direct me to Dad's room in the oncology wing anymore. I know its location by heart now: third floor, turn right twice, last door on the left, number 302. Too impatient to wait for the elevator, I take the stairs two at a time.

As I open the door, I suck in a breath when I catch sight of Dad. Even after visiting him half a dozen times in the past two weeks, it's still scary to see him in such grave condition. The friendly giant of my childhood, the wise, gentle god who always knew exactly what to do, now lies pale and haggard in a hospital bed with a dizzying array of tubes and wires and beeping machines all around him. His mortality stalks closer and closer, slow but inexorable—it doesn't need to hurry, because it knows it will catch its prey in the end—and I have no choice but to stare the beast right in its bloodshot, jaundiced eye.

*I hate this.*

I want to fix every single thing, make all his pain and sickness go away.

But I'm powerless.

When I sit in the single chair at his bedside, Dad stirs and his eyes drift open. He sits up with a slight effort. "Olivia . . . how are you, sweetheart?" Maybe it's just my imagination, but his voice sounds a little hoarse.

A gloomy laugh vomits up my throat. He's lying here looking so weak, and he's asking me how *I* am? "Never mind, that's not important. Are you okay? What happened? How long do they think you're going to be here?"

The spot where he split his head and needed stitches is now just a faint line above his eyebrow. It's healed nicely. But it's the stuff inside that counts. That's where the sickness I can't see or fight lurks.

"Slow down, sweetie, one question at a time. I just had another little dizzy spell. Probably from the chemotherapy more than the cancer itself. And they don't know yet; they're still running tests. I swear those vampires have sucked out half my blood. But the doctor said it could be anywhere from a couple more weeks all the way to . . ."

I swallow past the lump in my throat. Dad lets his sentence trail off, but I know what he would have said. *All the way to the end.*

Dad shifts a little to lay his clammy hand over mine. "Now, tell me how things are going with you."

Stubborn old man. But if he wants a distraction, I guess I can't blame him. And it'll probably ease his mind to hear about our good fortune. I tug my cardigan over my shoulders since the air-conditioning in this place is always set to frigid, and I lean in closer to Dad.

"I'm not quite done running the numbers yet . . ." Before everything went totally off the rails today, my plan was to finalize everything by lunchtime. "But I think we're pretty much back on track. My projections have been looking better than ever. I'd say things are in the bag."

The board meeting isn't for another few days, so their decision still remains to be seen, but barring any random disasters, Tate & Cane will almost certainly be safe from their swinging ax.

Dad interrupts my thoughts with a gravelly chuckle. "That's not what I meant, sweetheart. I wanted to know how *you* are."

*Oh.* It takes me a moment to process the question. "I'm fine," I say with a confused shrug. Exhausted from pulling two weeks of crazy overtime and weak from panic over Dad's health, sure ... but a good night's sleep can take care of that. Or the former problem, at least. "Why do you ask?" Surely he has more important things to worry about.

"Because you're my daughter, and no matter what happens, you'll always be my baby girl. And because you don't sound so sure. Are you happy? How are things with Noah?"

Oh fuck. I have no idea. Where do I even begin?

"I guess ... I don't know," I admit.

"Still?" His eyebrow raises.

"What with your health and all the craziness at work lately, I haven't exactly had much time to focus on my own life," I say, defending myself. And Dad's latest episode has driven everything else straight out of my head.

"That's no reason to put yourself last, sweetheart. Someday I'll be gone, and success comes and goes on its own schedule, but you're the only *you* you've got. And love . . . if you nurture it well, love will always be there to keep you strong. So it's important to take time to put your own house in order."

His words hit me square in the chest. Helpless to disagree, I nod. "Okay, Dad. I promise I'll work on it."

Not to mention the fact that he's right, of course. I can't avoid it any longer. This uncertainty about our relationship has been eating me up inside. And no amount of throwing myself into work has helped.

"That's my smart girl. Now, go ahead and get on with your day. I'll be all right without you hovering over me." He winks at me and I smile despite myself.

With another squeeze of his hand, I kiss him on the cheek and shake my head. "If you don't mind, I think I'll stay for a couple hours, Dad. Work can wait."

The need to be in his presence, to hear his soft breathing, to smell his musky soap smell is almost a physical ache. I don't even want to think about the fact that there will come a time when I can no longer have those things.

He nods. "Fine by me, sweetie."

• • •

Later, on my way back from the hospital to the office building, orange construction signs block the road I normally take. I haul the steering wheel over with a growl to find another route. Today, of all possible days, is when the city finally gets off its ass and fixes potholes? Sweet Jesus, I don't have time for this crap—

Well, really, I have plenty of time. It's just the patience I don't have. One more thing and my hair might catch fire from stress.

Manhattan's maze of one-way streets forces me to take a wide detour. Waiting at a red light that's so long I swear it must be broken, I drum my fingers on the steering wheel, looking around the street just to pass the time. I don't often come to this precise part of town.

Although . . .

*Huh, that tea shop looks familiar.*

A slow smile uncurls on my lips. It's the place where I bought Noah our Japanese teapot as a housewarming gift. I still remember that night, the first in our new shared penthouse. The teapot was a peace offering. An acknowledgment that we weren't in harmony yet, but we could get there if we tried—and I was willing to try.

God, and I'd been so nervous that night. Moving into a shiny new penthouse apartment with a man as gorgeous and sexy and bold as Noah. When I remember the careful way he agreed to go slow and nurtured a tender make-out session between us, it seems almost comical.

Warmth floods my chest and I have to laugh out loud. *I kept totally missing the picture, so fate had to smack me in the face with it.* It's almost ironic that such a simple coincidence tells me what I should have realized so long ago.

I'm in love with Noah.

Somewhere between our shared childhoods and the first time we slept together, I fell hard for that wonderful, maddening, passionate man, with no hope of ever coming back. And even when I was so angry at Noah I could spit, I was still in love with him. *I guess Dad was right about love always being there . . . although that's probably not the way he meant it.*

But my euphoria soon deflates. No matter what I feel, I still don't know where we stand. No matter how generously I try to see things from his perspective, no matter how many times he says he made a horrible mistake and he'll never, ever do it again, nothing can erase the fact that he lied to me. He withheld vital information from me in order to control how I feel about him.

*I didn't tell you something awkward because I was afraid to lose you* is an understandable human weakness, but it's still manipulative. And the memory of seeing him in our bathroom with that needle still gives me goosebumps.

So even if I do love him, I have no idea what to do with this information. Or even what I *want* to do. My heart is still split between hating Noah and missing him, so badly it feels like a piece of me has been torn out.

I let out a huff of frustration. Whenever we're together, I immediately find myself gravitating toward him as if nothing bad ever happened between us. Our attraction is a force of nature. Opposite magnetic poles that have always been, and will always be, drawn together.

And it's not just my body—although God knows I can't keep my hands off him, no matter how hard I try. Our minds and personalities fit into each other's gaps. Our business strategies weren't quite enough on their own, but when united, they pulled the company out of the red. And when I was suddenly called away from the party, I automatically trusted Noah to handle everything. Me, the control freak who took forever to learn how to unclench and delegate to her own best friend.

We complete each other. So perfectly, I can't help but wonder . . .

Maybe there's a way we can make this work after all.

For the past several weeks, I've been doing what I

always do in hairy social situations—repressing the hell out of my emotions by immersing myself in work, like an ostrich burying her head in the sand. I had hoped that, with enough time and space, my feelings would naturally settle enough to let me articulate and sort through them.

But that tactic clearly hasn't worked. Putting my emotions on ice was just a poor excuse for procrastination—it wasn't a real problem-solving strategy. I just didn't want to deal with the problem at all. A relationship isn't the kind of thing that can solve itself with a little percolating. *Geez, this marriage thing is hard.*

And my other favorite strategies won't work, either. I can be hyper-logical and organized, I can list pros and cons all day, and it still won't help me get to the heart of the matter. Everything ultimately boils down to my choice. My messy, scary, no-safety-net choice.

*If I love him . . . will I wind up hurt one day?*

I hate how vague and painful everything feels. I'm so used to cold, hard numbers, to having something objective to grasp onto, to letting facts and figures and statistics point me toward the right answer, or at least help guide me part of the way. Now, I'm all on my own.

Well, actually, I'm not. I have a partner in all of this. Which is part of the problem, but also part of the solution.

Complete forgiveness is one thing; I still don't know if I'm ready for that. But right this moment, all I really need is closure. I need some sense of where we're headed, because I can't stand living in this awkward limbo any longer. I can't go about my daily life, trying not to look at or touch the man whose workplace I share all day and whose bed I share all night. Sleeping curled up tight, facing opposite directions, the few feet between us feeling like a frigid mile.

We can't keep drifting through this uncomfortable space, peering nervously over the edge of the rift between us, waiting for something to either drag us away or tip us into the abyss. We need to take a step under our own power. We need to hash things out and make a well-considered decision that we can stick to.

As for what that decision might be . . .

I don't want to end our relationship. The only alternative is to continue it, and that will take a leap of faith. Would it really be the end of the world if I gave Noah another chance?

I almost have to smile. Yet another trial period—our relationship seems to have a pattern going here. Although this one might be the most important of all. Can Noah transition from my crush to my frenemy to my happily-ever-after?

No, I'm getting ahead of myself. All I know for sure is that we need to have a long conversation tonight.

I turn my car toward home, intent on doing just that. But part of me still hopes that maybe, just maybe … some things really are that simple. Or at least, simpler than they've seemed lately.

# Chapter Ten

*Noah*

Olivia's been under an enormous amount of stress lately, even more so than normal. In addition to running a business, and tiptoeing around our fragile, still-healing relationship, she's been faced with her father's fading health.

For a long time, we've all pretended he could plug on forever. But the truth is, he's not fine. His prognosis is grim, and it's possible he won't leave the hospital this time. I wish more than anything that I could fix this, that I could steal Olivia away and shield her from all the pain to come.

Between us, we've already lost three parents; this shouldn't be new territory. But the thing is, you never get used to it. You can never truly prepare your heart for that empty space that will ache without any cure.

I sigh and rise from the couch. Olivia will be home soon, and I plan to have dinner waiting for her. If there's even a small way I can improve her day, of course I'm going to do it.

I sauté tomatoes and garlic with white wine and have a pot of linguine boiling away when I hear the door open.

"Hello?" Olivia calls.

"In the kitchen." I finish slicing a loaf of crusty bread and turn off the burners just as Olivia enters the room.

She offers me a sad smile. I know that visiting her dad takes a toll on her. In that moment, I decide she won't go see him again without me by her side. Even though she's never admitted it, maybe being alone at the hospital isn't so good for her. I should be there when she needs someone to lean on, someone to vent to.

Her feet are bare, which means she's a good seven inches shorter than me, and I pull her in close for a hug. After living together for the past couple of months, I've learned that she always immediately deposits those torture devices she calls shoes by the front door, to be carried lovingly to her closet later. She looks great in heels, but I make a mental note to give her a foot massage later.

Olivia rests her head against my chest. "I was thinking . . . we should talk."

I nod. "Yes, but first, carbs."

She chuckles. "You know me too well."

Olivia grabs plates and napkins and sets the table while I drain the pasta and toss it in the homemade sauce, adding plenty of grated parmesan cheese.

We enjoy dinner with a glass each of chilled white wine on the couch, while the TV plays softly in the background. It feels so domestic and normal.

After we finish up, I watch Olivia carry the plates to the kitchen. She's tossed her hair up into a messy bun atop her head, and though she's still in her work clothes—a sleek black pencil skirt and cream-colored silk blouse with little buttons at the neckline—she looks casual and relaxed.

As I watch her pour us each another glass of wine, two things hit me simultaneously—I'm in love with her, and I can't continue like this. I can't have her in bits and pieces, groveling for her attention, living and working beside her like I'm unaffected, and then fucking her in a frenzy when she deems it okay. I don't want her scraps; I want her everything.

When she sits back down beside me, I'm prepared to lay it all out on the line. To tell her that we've reached the end of the road, and it's time for her to decide—all or nothing, winner take all. But Olivia beats me to the punch.

"I've been thinking a lot about us lately," she says, her voice unsure. She swallows and sets her wineglass down on the coffee table beside mine.

"And what have you been thinking?" I turn toward her on the sofa, encouraging her to continue.

"I can't do this anymore." She shakes her head as if she's clearing an unpleasant thought.

My stomach drops. Like I'm free-falling, plummeting toward disaster with no way to stop it.

"I hate not knowing where we stand, what might happen next." She twists her hands in her lap, looking uncomfortable.

"And what do you want to happen next?" I almost hold my breath as I wait for her answer.

"I just want . . . things to be better. Like they were before. I . . . I was falling in love with you, Noah," she stammers.

*Love.* My heart leaps. Not so long ago, it was a four-letter word that would have sent me running. But here and now, falling from Olivia's perfect lips . . . I've never heard a sweeter sound. I want to seize her in my arms, kiss her hard, pleasure her right here on the sofa. Show her just how badly I've missed her.

But I tamp down my excitement and force myself to tread carefully. We're not out of the woods quite yet.

I interlace our fingers and tug her closer. "Then don't stop."

Olivia's gaze lifts to mine. "I'm scared."

"I am too," I admit. We both understand that whatever happens next, we're in this together. And it will be with two hearts fully on the line, instead of just our jobs. That seems so much more fragile and real that I imagined it would.

"What does this mean?" she asks.

I pull her even closer, so she's practically in my lap. Stroking her cheek with my fingertips, I press a soft, chaste kiss to her mouth. "It means that we're in this together, for real this time, as husband and wife. No do-overs, no matter what. I don't care what happens to the company . . . all I want is you. I want your days and your nights and everything in between. I can't bear the thought of not having you. I want to be the man to hold you through all of life's ups and downs."

And there will be plenty, make no mistake. We've weathered a lot of storms together already, but we're both mature enough to know we're probably not through the worst of it yet. But that's exactly why I want to be her safe and steady place.

A sad smile forms on her lips. "I want that too."

"And I'm so fucking sorry about not telling you about the heir clause. I swear I never—"

She holds up her hand, waving off my umpteenth

apology. "I know, Noah. Please don't. We don't need to rehash it. If we do this, *if* we move forward, I want you to know I promise not to bring up your mistakes and hold them over your head."

I nod. "Thank you. That's more than I deserve." And just one more reason why she's the perfect woman, though I don't like that she said the word *if*. For me, there are no ifs. I'm already too deep in love to hold anything back. She cradles my heart in her hands, and all I can do is wait for her decision.

"But this baby business . . ." She chews on her lower lip, her eyes searching mine. "A baby is something we'll have to talk about. It's something that won't come until later. *Much* later . . . if at all. I'm still processing that."

My heart jumps into my throat. The thought of Olivia round with my child makes me feel almost dizzy. Knowing that there's a possibility down the road, that it's a choice we might make together . . . that's everything to me.

"That's fine," I say, trying to keep cool. "I just want us to be a couple. It's all I've ever wanted—a real shot with you. I know we entered into this marriage under unusual circumstances, but to me, it's not a fake marriage. It never was." I lean in and give her another kiss, tender and soft.

"What are you saying?" She pulls back to gaze at me quizzically.

I shrug. "When Sterling expected me to be freaked out about getting hitched, I wasn't. And when everyone thought I'd get cold feet, I didn't. You're all I've ever wanted. The one girl who seemed to be immune to my charms, the one person who could keep me on my toes, debating with me for hours. The most beautiful woman who I always desired, yet never got a shot with. You're mine now, and now that I've got you, I won't mess this up. I promise you."

"Noah . . ." She makes a soft sound of approval.

"From now on, everything is going to be fifty-fifty. I promise to communicate with you openly and honestly. I promise to include you, no matter how unpleasant the situation. We're partners in crime. Till the end. Please, you can't go. I love you."

She chews on her lip, keeping me in agony. Then she smiles. "I'm not going anywhere. I love you too."

My lips crash down onto hers. I'm so full of every emotion all at once—love, lust, happiness—I feel like I could burst. I lift her from the couch and carry her to our bedroom.

The room we've shared in stony silence for the past three weeks is silent no more, because the moment Olivia's placed in the center of the bed, I pull her skirt and panties down in one quick tug, and a surprised gasp pushes past her lips. Next comes her shirt, followed by her lacy bra.

"Hey there, tiger." She grins at me with a hunger that makes my cock twitch. "Let's even things up."

I strip my shirt off over my head while Olivia's deft fingers go to work on my belt. And then I'm lying beside my wife, her warm skin on mine, her kisses on my throat, and everything is right with the world.

We kiss for a long time. I feel like I can't get enough of her, enough of her honeysuckle scent, her soft breathy moans. But the need to be closer to her—

to be inside her, to possess her—wins out.

"Need to make love to you," I murmur against her lips. It's the first time I've spoken those words to a woman. *Make love.* But, I realize, that's exactly what this is.

"Yes," she whispers.

Reaching over toward the nightstand, I grab a condom from the drawer. Then, upon further consideration, I go back and grab a second one and toss them on the bed beside us.

Olivia chuckles. "Someone's ambitious tonight."

Damn straight I am. I've waited too long to have her. If I've done my job properly, she'll be sore and tired come morning.

I rip open the package but Olivia takes over the task of sheathing me, her hands gentle and much softer than mine would have been. My need to be closer to her overtakes every other instinct, as if this union is more significant than all the other times she's given herself to me combined.

Our previous intimate encounters were all born out of deceit. Yes, she was willing, but tonight she's committed. She's given me her heart, forgiven all my transgressions, and the desire to show her just what that means to me is an unmistakable need. She's not my girlfriend or fake fiancée or the other half of my arranged marriage. She's my *wife*. And I have a feeling that getting her to understand that fact is going to take more work, but in this moment, all I'm interested in is making her feel good.

I pull Olivia up so she's straddling my hips. And then I guide her up, aligning myself with her. When she sinks down, it's heaven. *Heaven.* Her head drops back and she releases a slow, low moan.

"Forever." I groan, gripping her hips tight as I control our pace. Nice and slow, so I can savor every breath, every moan, every squeeze of her inner muscles.

"Noah," she whispers, placing her hands on my abs as she urges me to pick up the pace. "Faster. More."

"Give it to me." I thrust up, claiming her.

"It's yours." She presses back down on me, so

deep.

My chest fills with love for this amazing woman, and I'm overcome by emotion. Burying myself in her over and over again affirms everything that is right about our union.

"Mine," I growl out.

"Always." She sobs, already breathless from pleasure.

*Always.*

# Chapter Eleven

*Olivia*

"In summation, it would be in the best financial interests of the board to retain Tate & Cane Enterprises," I finish breathlessly, glancing at Noah. "How was that?"

"Great. I think we've got this." He gives me a weary smile. "Like I said after our last two practice runs."

I chew my lip, which I've already bitten raw over the course of the night. "Should we rehearse one more time? I don't know if my delivery is as convincing as it could be. And maybe I should make those extra slides I was talking about earlier. Our argument could always stand to be stronger—"

Noah reaches out to squeeze my shoulder, both to interrupt me and to reassure me. "Snowflake. Calm down. Our presentation is fine. And it's one in the morning—I'm exhausted and I'm sure you are too. At this point, getting a good night's sleep will do more to help our argument than a hundred graphs."

"Okay, okay." I sigh in defeat. Just the mention of the word *sleep* triggers a yawn.

"See? Let me take you to bed."

My lips quirk and I raise my eyebrow at him slightly. "What's with that tone? I thought you wanted sleep."

He smiles back. "Don't worry; I do. Sex can wait until tomorrow night, after we've kicked ass with our presentation and saved the world."

Another yawn interrupts my chuckle as Noah leads me to bed.

• • •

That night, still laughing in triumph, we pile through our penthouse's front door like a couple of college kids who just graduated.

"We did it! We saved our whole fucking company!" I whoop aloud, kicking off my heels. Even after all our hard work, I can still barely believe we convinced the board to let Tate & Cane live. Although the unfulfilled heir clause lost us our shares, we still have our jobs as the head of the company. We can still live our legacy, and really that's all we ever wanted.

"Damn right we did. We were unstoppable in there." Noah lifts me by the waist and spins me around the entry hall, making me squeal in surprise and delight. "And it was your brilliant party idea that saved our asses, Snowflake."

"Don't even try to act so modest. I couldn't have managed that horrible mountain of work without you." I playfully slap at his shoulders—the only part of him I can reach in this position. "Now, put me down so you can pour us some drinks."

"Another great idea. I'll crack open a nice cold bottle of champagne." Noah sets me back on my feet, shucks his suit jacket, and tosses it over the back of a chair.

"You already have one chilled?" I ask, following him into the kitchen.

"Last night I figured if we won, we'd want to

celebrate, and if we lost, we'd want to drown our sorrows."

"What a vote of confidence. You should have told me that you were sure we'd win."

He shrugs, giving me a crooked smile. "Yeah, but we did win, right?"

I take two flutes down from the cupboard while Noah gets the champagne from the fridge and uncorks it. There's something magical about the sound of a champagne bottle popping—it feels like a mini celebration in and of itself. Noah pours both our flutes full to the brim.

"To success in business, to victories hard won . . . and to unstoppable couples," he says, raising his glass into the air.

"To all that stuff." I pick up my flute, clink it against his, and take a long sip, relishing the sweet bubbles bursting over my tongue.

"Now, where's my congratulatory kiss?"

Rolling my eyes, I lean in and give him a peck on

the lips. He lets out a low murmur of appreciation and tries to pull me in closer, but I draw back.

"That was it?" he protests.

"Let me at least get through a single glass of champagne first. I'm not done savoring our triumph yet."

When we polish off our first glasses, Noah pours us both another round. "What should we toast to this time?"

"Hmm," I say thoughtfully. "You covered a lot in our first toast. How about . . . to marrying well?"

Noah blinks at me, then nods, a grin slowly spreading over his face. "I like that one."

I clink glasses with a smile of my own. I guess I surprised him. But he, and all the joy he brings me, surprised me first.

Noah ends his drink by heaving a satisfied sigh. "This is great."

I nod emphatically. "I know. God, it feels so amazing not to have the board's decision hanging over our head anymore."

"Well, that too." He beams at me. "But I was also talking about spending time at home with you. I can't think of the last time we just hung out and had fun like this."

Our separation wasn't only because we've been so busy with work. I also wasn't sure quite where we stood, and struggled to get my footing under me with this relationship. But all that pain is in the past—we talked over our feelings, we said all the things we needed to say, and now we're trying to leave the whole ugly episode behind us.

Sensing my hesitation, Noah reaches out to lace his fingers through mine. "Sorry, I didn't mean to be a buzzkill there. I just meant that . . . well, I'm glad to see you happy again."

Holding my gaze, he raises my hand to his lips and kisses my knuckles with a smile, just like he did on the day I first agreed to date him. That fateful meeting wasn't even three months ago, but it feels like a lifetime—maybe because I've become a different person. Whoever could have thought that our relationship would blossom like this? If someone had told me then that I'd fall ass over teakettle in love with Noah Tate, I might have slapped them. I'd have been scandalized.

In a huskier tone, Noah adds, "Speaking of having fun . . . Come here, beautiful."

The heat in his dark eyes chases all other thoughts out of my head. "Okay, but I want to try something new tonight."

His interest deepens. "Oh?"

I reach out to grasp his necktie. His breathing quickens as I undo the knot and slip the long ribbon of wine-red silk from his shirt collar.

"I want you to blindfold me," I say, feeling my cheeks turn a little pink despite myself. I'll have to get used to talking about stuff like this if I'm going to be married to a sex god.

His eyes widen, in disbelief as well as excitement. "Are you sure?"

"Yes. I trust you."

And I want to *show* him that I trust him. I'm not nearly as good with words as he is, but with this act—putting my body and my pleasure squarely into his hands—I know my meaning will come through, more strongly than just telling him that I forgive him.

When Noah kisses me, hard and deep and so heartfelt, it makes my eyes sting with happy tears. It's clear that he understands.

We're both a little breathless by the time he pulls back. Without a word, he takes my hand and leads me down the hallway. Once we're in the bedroom, he turns again to face me, still holding my hand.

"Let me undress you," he says, his voice already a little husky.

Swallowing hard, I nod.

With a slowness that seems part reverence and part just teasing me with anticipation, he strips me out of my office clothes. First my blouse, button by button, then my skirt, unzipped and slid down my legs. He kisses me as he reaches around my back to unclasp my bra. My panties are the last to go.

Finally, I stand naked before him. Tonight, with Noah, I can take a break from being a high-powered executive. Right now I'm just Olivia—a woman ready and waiting for her husband's touch.

He nudges me back to lie down on the bed, then sits beside me and knots his necktie around my head to cover my eyes. All I can see is a thin sliver of light at the bottom of my makeshift blindfold. I feel the bed dip as he kneels over me, bracing himself on his hands so that our only point of contact is the occasional brush of his cotton dress slacks on my legs.

For a moment, there's only the faint hush of our breathing. Then Noah's mouth ghosts over the shell of my ear and I sigh aloud.

He starts kissing down my body, taking his time with every sensitive area as if he's savoring my taste. Not being able to predict his movements makes every touch a delightful surprise. Not being able to watch him work is a different kind of sweet torture—I wish I could see his full lips on my skin, his eyes lit up with fiery desire.

I make up for it with my hands. I bury my fingers

in his messy hair, enjoying its texture and the way his breath hitches whenever I tug a little too hard in my excitement. I stroke his shoulders and back just to feel his skin and the firm muscles moving under it. I want to learn every inch of him. Maybe we should do this again sometime, but with him wearing the blindfold . . .

Teeth scrape gently over the spot on my neck that always turns my knees to jelly. Soft, full lips brush my collarbone, my upper chest, then the very top of my breast, inching lower, lower. My stomach flutters with eagerness. His touch is traveling down so slowly, I feel like I might explode from sheer anticipation. Jesus, is he planning on keeping up this pace all night?

Heat throbs straight to my clit when he finally seals his mouth over one nipple, licking and sucking hard, pinching and rolling my other nipple between his thumb and finger.

"Noah," I say on a moan, pleading. My hips lift in rhythm with the writhing of his tongue. I'm so wet already; I can feel the slickness between my legs every time I squirm. And if I raise my knee, I can feel him too, a steel bar straining against the zipper of his dress slacks.

I rub my knee against his hardness and smirk when I hear a groan.

"Tonight's supposed to be about you." He sounds a lot more turned on than annoyed.

I reach out and hear him suck in his breath when my fingers close around his erection. "But *this* is for me, isn't it? So, what's the problem?"

"Naughty girl," he growls. "Do I have to stop and tie you up? Or can you be good?"

I shake my head. "I don't know about *good*, but I'll be patient, if that's what you want." For at least a little longer, anyway. I don't know how much more of this teasing I can take.

"But I'm not going to stop touching my husband's big, sexy cock, so don't even ask." I grin, unable to help myself.

He kisses the smile right off my lips. "You can touch me anywhere you want, *after* you come for me."

*After?* I like the sound of that . . . but damn, how long will I have to wait?

Without more dialogue on the subject, he switches breasts—his fingers slipping and sliding over the nipple he was licking before, his lips and tongue and teeth almost too intense on the one that his fingers pinched into turgid stiffness. Then he resumes his journey south. My belly jumps ticklishly with every kiss.

I gasp and twitch in anticipation at a sudden puff of air on my center. Fabric rasps quietly—he's scooting down over the sheets. Then I feel his lips brush my ankle.

"Y-you suck." I giggle helplessly. He's really skipping over the main attraction? After starting at my ears and working all the way down, he's going to start over again at my feet and work up too? *Geez* . . .

"It'll all be worth it, I promise," he purrs, his hot breath fanning over my calf.

I try to force myself to hold still as his mouth travels slowly up my legs. But a ragged moan bursts from my throat when he starts sucking and biting at my inner thighs. I'd never let Noah hear the end of it if he ever left a hickey on my neck, but nobody else will ever see these marks. They're private, intimate, their sensual meaning reserved for us and us alone. And the idea that Noah is claiming me as his own . . . it makes me shiver almost as much as the sensation of his love bites themselves.

His large, warm hands grip my thighs and spread them. I shudder at the feel of his breath ghosting over my wet pussy again. Why isn't he moving?

"W-what are you doing?" I groan.

"Just pausing to admire you."

My cheeks heat up. I'm not ashamed of my body, but he's talking about my lady parts like he's looking at a work of art or something.

"Is it really that—?"

"Beautiful, yes."

The urge to clamp my thighs together flares up, but I fight internally with myself to let him *admire* me.

"Hot." He kisses the very top of my mound once. "Tight." His mouth moves lower, an innocent kiss placed a fraction lower. "Sweet." Another kiss, another tiny, maddening step closer to where I want him. "Wet."

I almost scream when his tongue finally, *finally* slides over my clit.

"Mine," he growls.

Noah licks and sucks with the same maddening leisure as when he worshiped my body. He doggedly ignores my fingers tangling in his hair and yanking his face into my core, trying to get him to hurry the fuck up already. But he's in no hurry to make me come. It's as if he has all day.

His hot, wet, agile tongue keeps flicking from side to side like a lazy swish of a cat's tail. It's exactly the sensation that gets me off best—if it were only a little bit faster. The blissful heat builds steadily, but goddammit, so *slowly*. I can feel the edge approaching, yet I can't quite reach it. All I can do is be patient and wait for Noah to take me there. This snail's pace is driving me crazy. Closer, closer, inch by inch . . .

Until he groans against my wet flesh and pushes a rigid finger into me. My climax finally breaks, flooding my body like an ocean of warm light, and it goes on and on and *on, fuck* . . .

I hear whimpering and realize it's me. His tongue keeps lashing over my clit, letting me ride out my orgasm to the very end, through the very last drops of pleasure.

I melt bonelessly into the sheets. As I drift down from my high, still loopy from the intensity, I let out a giggle. Everything about this day—triumph for our families' company, peace and love in our marriage—has been such a long time coming. I guess it's only fitting that my orgasm would be an exercise in patience too.

The bed dips again as his weight and body heat leave me for a moment. The rattle of a drawer sliding open, followed by a crinkle of plastic, tells me he's putting on a condom.

I want to rip off the blindfold, see his dilated pupils, his swollen lips, his rock-hard, dripping cock. But then he moves over me and kisses me hard as the blunt head of his cock nudges my pussy lips.

I suck in my breath when he begins to enter me— so slowly, pulls out, and pushes back in, letting me adjust to his size again. Even though I'm slick from my orgasm, it's still a tight fit. It probably always will be. *To marrying well, indeed.*

With everything that's been on my plate lately, we haven't had sex in almost a week—and that's a week too long, as far as I'm concerned. I'm so damn ready for this.

I rock my hips up, panting, "Please, Noah, fuck me."

He makes a quiet, rough noise of desire. "Jesus, Snowflake, how could any man say no to that?"

A deep moan of relief escapes me as he starts thrusting in earnest. Every stroke pounds straight into my G-spot, sending shock waves of pleasure through my entire body, still oversensitive from my last orgasm. Sex while blindfolded is a totally different experience. I'm hyper-attuned to his every rough breath, every thrust of his hips, every rigid vein and ridge in his large cock.

I grope around the sheets for Noah's hand, find it, and squeeze tight after he laces our fingers together—an anchor in the sea of sensation that rocks me. His lips press against mine and I open hungrily to his kiss. My tongue reaches out for his and intertwines, a sweet, hot dance that echoes the movements of our bodies. We only break apart to gasp for breath, dizzy with exertion and each other.

"I thought I was going to lose you," Noah groans into my ear.

I arch my hips up and tighten my legs around his waist, needing him deeper, needing to hold him close. "You've got me now," I pant. "I love you, Noah . . . so much."

And I want more. We move together almost frantically, rushing to meet each other, pleasure building with every rocking thrust.

When it comes, my second orgasm doesn't wash over me like a gentle sea. It shudders through me as violently as an earthquake, a lightning strike, locking my muscles and pulling a tight cry from my throat. Somewhere in the maelstrom of pleasure, I feel Noah shudder around me, inside me, moaning my name like a prayer.

I fall limp, my legs still draped around his waist.

Our harsh panting and the smell of sweat and sex hang heavy in the air. When he eases out of me, I feel a little empty, but mostly just exhausted and satisfied. I hear the sound of latex unpeeling from skin, followed by the rustle of a plastic trash bag as Noah throws away the condom.

His muscled arms reach out and pull me against his hot chest, still damp with sweat. With a quiet murmur, I turn on my side to pillow my head on his firm bicep. Gingerly, I stretch out my tired legs. My muscles will definitely be sore tomorrow, but damn, this is so worth it.

Light floods back into my world as Noah removes my blindfold. I squeeze my eyes shut, both because the sudden brightness stings and because I want to hold on to this moment for just a little longer.

"How was that?" he asks. "From all the noise you made, it sounded like it felt good."

"Amazing." I sigh, already slipping into drowsiness. I'm too wiped out to worry about my honesty overinflating his ego.

But Noah doesn't brag or tease me. He just kisses my forehead in soft affection. "I'm glad you liked it. And by the way, I love you more."

I curve my arm around his trim waist. Cuddled close, we rest in each other's embrace, bathed in a warm glow of contentment.

I can hardly believe things are going so well. Just a few weeks ago, our relationship teetered on the brink. Now we're stronger than ever. A real couple. I couldn't be happier, and if tonight was any indication, he feels the same way.

# Chapter Twelve

*Noah*

At the flurry of noise and people rushing past my office door, I stand up to peek out into the hall. I've had my head down most of the morning, reviewing the pitch campaigns created by the marketing team for all our new accounts. It's good to be busy again with the influx of so many new clients.

I stop at my assistant's desk. "What's going on?"

Her gaze follows the crowd to where they stand, necks craned, watching the flat-screen perched on the wall in the break room just down the hall. "Have you seen the news?" she asks.

I give my head a shake, and she taps her computer monitor with one long, lacquered fingernail. "It's Daniels Multimedia, one of the companies who wanted to buy us out. The heir to the company, Bradford Daniels . . . he's all they're talking about today."

"That pencil dick," I utter under my breath.

"What's he done now?"

Margot blushes at my vulgar language. She's sixty-eight and retiring in two weeks. I don't know what I'm going to do without her. I've brought in dozens of applicants, and so far there hasn't been even one I'd consider.

I need someone capable, trustworthy, and according to my wife, someone who isn't interested in fucking me. Olivia's vetoed nearly every candidate.

Margot opens her browser and the CNN headline reads Junior Executive Exposed in Sex, Money Scandal!

I lean over her shoulder, skimming the article to discover that mega-douche Brad got caught with his pants down. He was blackmailing his assistant, a single mom and longtime faithful employee. When she discovered he was embezzling funds and hiding the money in an offshore account, he made her an offer. He promised her a promotion as long as she didn't say anything. But she couldn't live with that and told his father what he was doing. Apparently, the stolen money was used to pay for his Internet porn addiction, among other things. The assistant reported that she'd walked in on him masturbating in his office several times.

*Hallelujah.* I love it when bad things happen to bad people. Especially since any lawyer worth their salt will find a way to tack on sexual harassment and creating a hostile work environment in addition to blackmail and embezzlement. The bastard will be looking at serious jail time.

Grabbing my phone, I dial Olivia.

But I can't even get past *hello* before she blurts, "Did you hear?" Her voice is almost giddy with disbelief.

"Yeah. This is just not his month."

"Oh, trust me, he deserves every bit of this."

Nodding, I head toward her office. When I arrive in front of her door, she looks up and stifles a giggle before hanging up the phone.

"Lunch?" I ask.

Her gaze lowers to the clock. It's before noon, but now that I've taken a break, I don't want to go back to my desk.

"Sure." She smiles at me again and rises from her desk.

I love that Brad has fallen from grace, but even more, I love how it's merely a blip on our radar. We've moved on, as individuals and as a couple, and his presence in our lives is insignificant. That's not to say we won't enjoy hearing the news once in a while, but it won't absorb us. This is our story, and it's one he has no part in anymore.

"Let's order in," I suggest, sinking into the plush seat across from her. "I've got another interview coming in at one today."

Olivia rolls her eyes. "I don't want to talk about that right now. I don't want to fight."

It's becoming a sore subject between us, which is unexpected. My wife is usually so self-confident; it's taken me by surprise that she has such an interest in who I hire to be my right hand.

My lips quirk. Maybe nobody will ever be good enough for her. Maybe this is how she shows her love—

by splashing her control-freakery all over me.

She cocks her head. "Something funny?"

I quickly school my features. "Just some dumb joke Sterling forwarded me this morning. I agree; let's have a nice lunch and not talk about business."

"What are you in the mood for?" she asks, pulling out a file folder containing paper menus from all the local eateries. Her dedication to organization no longer surprises me.

"You choose," I say with the wave of a hand. "Surprise me."

A surprise. *That's it.*

As Olivia pores over the various menus, I slide my phone out of my pocket and send a text to Camryn.

*NOAH: Meet me for an early happy hour today. I need your help.*

Camryn responds almost immediately.

CAMRYN: *You buying?*

NOAH: *Sure. 4 p.m. at Woody's Stiff Pickle.*

CAMRYN: *Sure thing, boss man.*

Her message ends with a thumbs-up emoji.

I put my phone away again, hiding my smirk. I know just what I need to do tonight to make sure Olivia never has to worry about this assistant business ever again.

• • •

"What's going on?" Camryn asks, taking a sip from her strawberry margarita.

We're seated at the bar. Woody's is a casual place, a sports bar with little ambience. But it's close to work, and more importantly, it's not somewhere Olivia would ever willingly set foot. So we're safe from being discovered.

"I need your help."

"Trouble in paradise? *Again?*" Camryn smirks at

me. "You're pretty efficient at fucking up; I'll give you that."

"Eh . . ." I tilt my hand from side to side. "It's not like that. Everything's actually going pretty well."

For a certain definition of the word, anyway. In itself, the assistant thing isn't a big deal; I know I'll figure it out eventually. But there's a lot going on in our world. Olivia's father's failing health, the idea of us maybe, someday having a baby, and of course, our new commitment to each other in this marriage.

"Everything's actually going well. I just . . . I want a do-over with Olivia."

"A do-over?" She drums her fingers on the bar. "What does that mean, exactly?"

"You're the one who told me Olivia was a closet romantic who'd always dreamed of a big, beautiful wedding."

"Well, yes." Camryn nods, her brunette waves bouncing. "That's true."

I almost cringe, thinking back on our wedding. If

you can even call that half-assed, clinical meeting a "wedding." We need a fresh start. I need to show Olivia everything she means to me. And a real wedding is going to be the first step toward doing that.

"So I need to plan one of those. A blow-out wedding like she's always wanted."

Camryn's lips quirk up. "Since you're already married, I'm guessing you mean a vow renewal."

"Sure. Doesn't matter what it's called. I need Olivia in a big poofy dress, a massive cake, our friends and families, great food, a band, and dancing under the stars."

Camryn's smile has bloomed into a full-on grin. "That's cute. You should totally do that. Can I be a bridesmaid?"

Now I'm the one smirking at her. "You said it's not a wedding. Do vow renewals even have a wedding party?"

"They do when you plan them."

I chuckle and take a sip of my beer. "I'm going to

need some help here. What did Olivia's dream wedding consist of? Can you remember anything from that scrapbook you mentioned?"

Camryn looks out over the bar, taking a moment to think. "You know what? No."

"Excuse me?" I'm taken aback.

She gives a flick of her wrist. "Those were her childhood dreams, the ramblings of an adolescent girl. Olivia's a woman now. And you know her better than anyone. You've got this."

How did I not know this was coming? Every time I've asked Camryn for help, she finds a way to make sure I'm forced to figure it out on my own.

"And besides, this . . ." She waves her hand in my direction. "This is amazing."

"What are you talking about?" I squint at her.

"A groom planning a vow renewal is about the sweetest, nicest thing ever. Go with it, trust your gut, and I'm sure Olivia will love it. It's inherently romantic because you're the one making an effort for her. That's what true love is all about, selflessly doing for another."

Before we get all mushy, I mutter a solemn, "Thanks."

Camryn just grins and takes another gulp of her drink.

"Check, please," I call to the bartender.

"Happy hour's over already?" she asks, pouting.

"Sorry to cut it short, but apparently I have an entire wedding to plan." I take the last swig from my beer bottle and rise to my feet.

"It's not a wedding. It's a vow renewal."

I roll my eyes. "Semantics." If it includes the wedding-night sex I never got, I'll be a happy man.

Plus I have another idea—a surprise for Olivia tonight that will prove to her she's the only woman in my life.

I slap down a couple of bills and tip my chin at Camryn. "Thanks for the chat."

She gives me a little wave as she polishes off her

margarita. "Anytime. Good luck."

• • •

Once Olivia gets home, it's our standard evening fare. Relaxing small talk, a light dinner enjoyed together at the table, and now, savoring a glass of wine in the living room. She's flipping through a stack of catalogs that came in the mail today. I shift on the couch, more nervous and excited than I realized I'd be.

"So, what were you up to this afternoon?" she asks.

I'd skipped out of work early to take care of a couple of things, telling Olivia I'd meet her at home.

"I had some business to take care of. I actually met Camryn for happy hour."

"Camryn? What for? Work stuff?"

I shake my head. "Personal stuff. I've been thinking about planning a do-over for our wedding. A real reception, all of it. Wanted to get her perspective on some things you might like."

She smiles tenderly, her gaze meeting mine. "That's awfully sweet of you, Mr. Tate."

"So you'd be game?" I trace my thumb over her jawline, and Olivia leans in to my touch.

"Of course." She presses a small kiss to my lips. "Did Camryn give you any ideas?"

I smirk. "Nope. She basically said I needed to figure it out on my own."

She chuckles. "That sounds like Camryn."

I pull Olivia closer on the couch. Lately every evening has ended with us making love, but for the last several nights, she's been distracted by thoughts of her dad and work, not one hundred percent in the mood. Tonight, I need to show her what a good stress relief fucking can bring.

"I've been thinking," she says, curling against my side.

"About?"

"I have an idea for replacement assistant."

"You do?"

I'm surprised to hear that Olivia's put more

thought into it. The control freak in her has been busy turning down every applicant who's walked through the door. Not that I've minded too much . . . it's cute to see her territorial side come out.

She lifts her head from my chest and nods. "Rosita would be perfect, Noah."

"Rosie?" My eyebrows dart up. "I love Rosie, but I doubt she's qualified." I reach across the table and take her hand. "Babe, you honestly have nothing to worry about. Even if I hired the world's hottest supermodel as my assistant, I'd still only have eyes for you."

"A supermodel wouldn't be qualified, either," she jokes. Then her smile softens, genuinely soothing. "I know. I mean, deep down, I do know that. And I trust you. It's just, I don't know . . . it's annoying to think that there are women out there who are only interested in sleeping their way to the top, who seduce the men they work for to get ahead."

I get what she's saying. Olivia has worked her ass off for every promotion she was awarded. It was due to skill and merit, not because of how short her skirt was or how low-cut her blouse. I can see that her anti-bimbo hiring practices have nothing to do with not trusting me and everything to do with her own personal code of ethics.

The significance of this conversation has taken a turn. I hadn't planned on showing her now, but what the hell—I need to prove to her that she owns me in every way possible. I start to unbutton my pants.

"I guess I shouldn't have gotten this, then . . ." I pull down the zipper and push down my boxers.

"Oh, for fuck's sake. What is with you and whipping out your . . . whoa!" Olivia slides from the couch and drops to her knees in front of me, inspecting my crotch with wide eyes. "What in the hell is that?"

The warning of the tattoo artist, the gun already buzzing in her hand, rings through my head. *Are you sure about this, buddy? You realize it's permanent.* Shit, maybe I have made a mistake . . .

Olivia plants her hands on my thighs and leans closer.

With her head practically in my lap, my dick starts to appreciate the attention, hardening and readying himself for action.

"What did you do?" she repeats.

The ink is still tender on my skin, and I probably shouldn't have removed that bandage, but I wanted her to be able to see.

Low on my groin, just above my junk, is written *Olivia Quinn Cane.*

I got it to cement my love for my wife, but since she's looking at me like I'm crazy, I'm not sure she appreciates the gesture. I scratch my head sheepishly.

"I know that was one of the things that bothered you when we first got together. You said I'd slept with half of Manhattan."

Olivia's eyes dart up to mine. "The female half, yes."

"And while that's not true, I got something today that I hope will show you I'm yours now. In every sense of the word."

She traces the gracefully lettered script. I bite my lip at her feather-light caress—the tattoo is still fresh enough to sting like a mofo, but my flesh also tingles at the gentle touch, so near my dick . . .

"I can't believe you put my name here," she murmurs.

I swallow hard, my voice husky with emotion as well as desire. "It's yours. I'm yours."

She climbs into my lap and kisses me deeply. "You're incredible. Crazy . . ." She chuckles. "But incredible."

"I love you."

"Love you more," she murmurs against my lips.

"Not possible."

I rise to my feet and carry her to the bedroom.

# Chapter Thirteen

*Olivia*

We waited to schedule our vow renewal until after Dad was released from the hospital into home hospice care. We also decided to hold it at the Cane family estate, where I grew up, so that he wouldn't have to travel anywhere. But Noah wouldn't let me do any of the planning beyond that, because he wanted everything to be a surprise.

Whatever he's concocting, I'm sure it'll be a far cry from the day we were legally married. That barely qualified as a wedding ceremony; it was only a legal union, just signing some papers. There was certainly nothing romantic about it. Today we'll be surrounded by a crowd of family and friends, all laughing, congratulating us, and toasting our happiness.

More importantly, I've come to grips with my feelings. I can look Noah in the eye and tell him I love him. I know exactly what my future holds, and I'm eager for every minute of it.

Well, the future in a general sense, anyway. Right now, I don't know anything, because Camryn is covering my closed eyes with her hands as she guides me through the house. She put on my makeup and helped me zip up my dress—a gorgeous pale pink princess-cut gown, boat neck with lacy cap sleeves—but she refused to breathe a single word about Noah's plans. I haven't even seen what she's wearing yet.

"Almost there," she says.

"I can tell."

I'm pretty sure where we are. The floor beneath my high heels has changed from the hardwood of the hallway into plush carpet, and I hear the buzzing murmur of our many guests talking, muffled by thick glass. We must be in the den, near the French doors that lead out onto the patio and rear garden.

"Don't open your eyes yet." Camryn's hands leave my face. A door handle clicks and the noise from the backyard abruptly becomes louder. "Okay, open them!"

The entire garden, already lovely in the golden light of late afternoon, is festooned with paper lanterns and garlands of fluffy peonies in every color of the rainbow. Each table holds its own small bouquet of peonies as a centerpiece. A bar and a long buffet table piled with what looks like tapas occupy the far right corner of the garden. On the opposite side, the same band we booked for Tate & Cane's big beach party provides a mellow instrumental backdrop.

And through the middle of the lawn, a snow-white runner marks the path to a tall, arched floral bower. Beneath it is an altar where we'll recite our renewed vows—and where Noah already stands, devastatingly handsome in his tuxedo, his glowing smile directed at me like I'm the only woman in the world.

My sister, Rachel, and a gaggle of my other female relatives encircle the patio. While I stand gawking at everything, they cheer at my approach, turning heads throughout the larger crowd and sparking off a round of applause. All the women are wearing identical tea-length tulle gowns in an airy shade of seafoam green, as if they were bridesmaids. And when I turn around in astonishment, I see that Camryn is dressed the same way too.

"You like it?" She laughs, pulling me into a hug. "Noah picked my brains about your perfect wedding. He must have sent me a million e-mails confirming everything."

Then the band starts playing the opening bars of the wedding march. The bridesmaids scatter to take their places along the aisle, and Camryn shoos me off, insisting, "Go on, you've got a husband to smooch!"

Blinking back tears of joy, I walk through my bridesmaids toward Noah. The man who so quickly became my friend, my groom, and finally my lover. Not the order that most people do romance in . . . but I wouldn't have things any other way, because this is *our* story.

As I reach the altar to stand at Noah's side, I spot Dad in his wheelchair at the very front of the audience, with an attending health aide sitting next to him. Of course I know that he's not well, but he's beaming like this is the best day of his life.

"You look stunning," Noah whispers to me, taking my hand and stroking the back of it. His eyes are shining like I've never seen.

The depth of emotion reflected back at me takes my breath away. I don't think his expression in this moment is something I'll ever forget for as long as I live. I feel like his entire world, his most important treasure, his everything. And I love it.

Noah turns to address our audience directly. "Three months ago, Olivia became my wife. But as many of you may know, our union was not a typical one. We married in stressful times; our families' company was facing the end of an era. And our relationship itself has had its share of rough spots. But we overcame every obstacle, and our love bloomed despite the circumstances."

Taking my hand, he turns to face me, still speaking clearly enough to let our guests hear. "You've made me a better man, Olivia. I believe in this marriage more than ever. I am so grateful that I get to spend the rest of my life at your side, and I eagerly await whatever that life may bring us."

My breath catches in my throat, but he's not done yet.

"On our wedding day, I pledged my commitment

to you. I promised to honor, cherish, and comfort you, in sickness and in health, for richer or poorer, for better or for worse. Now I want to add true love to that list. I am honored to stand here today, in front of these witnesses"—with his free hand, Noah makes a sweeping gesture that encompasses our entire audience—"not only to reaffirm all my wedding promises, but to announce that I love you. I always have and I always will, for as long as we both shall live."

Noah suddenly drops to one knee. "Will you take me as your husband again, Olivia?"

Blinking back tears, I take his hand and encourage him to his feet. I lift up on my toes and press a kiss to his lips.

"I do," I whisper against his mouth.

The crowd surrounding us bursts into a chorus of whoops, whistles, and applause. I glimpse Dad and several of the bridesmaids dabbing at their eyes.

Just as the sun touches the horizon, the paper lanterns blink to life, one by one, transforming the garden into an enchanting dance floor. The band eases down into a languid, soulful tune and the singer starts crooning "At Last" by Etta James.

Noah stands up, still holding my hand. "May I have this dance, Mrs. Tate?"

*Our first wedding dance . . . it might not be our first dance as a married couple, but it means the same thing.*

I step close to Noah and loop my arms around his neck. "Of course. Lead the way."

Gently rocking, wrapped warm in each other's embrace, we sway in slow circles around the dance floor. I rest my head on Noah's shoulder and enjoy the feeling of moving together with him, our rhythms united. We've spent our whole lives so close, but just barely out of step. Now we're finally in tune, in sync, in love.

When the song ends, it feels like waking up from a dream. Our guests applaud as we step off the dance floor and others step onto it, letting the reception officially begin.

A white-coated waiter serves us chilled glasses of champagne, each topped with a slice of floating strawberry.

We take a sip, and as the bubbles dance on my tongue, I find myself blinking back tears once again. The scene before me is almost too much. Every inch of this reception is beautiful. And all of it was planned for me by my husband. *Seriously, what guy does that?*

"What do you think?" Noah asks, dropping a tender kiss onto the back of my neck. "Is it everything you hoped it might be?"

"No." I shake my head. "It's more." My throat is tight, and I know he can see my eyes brimming with tears. I blink them away, refusing to ruin my makeup that Camryn spent an hour applying.

"I love you," he says simply.

We walk over toward our head table that faces out on the garden and all the guests.

"Why did you say no to me all those years ago?" I ask.

He looks at me quizzically. "When?"

"That summer at Puget Sound. I was ready to hand

you my virginity on a silver platter."

He laces his fingers with mine. "Because I knew back then I wasn't ready for a woman like you. You weren't the casual type. You were the marrying type. And I was still just a dumb kid—all I wanted to do was sow my wild oats. I didn't deserve the greatest gift you could offer."

His answer is so honest, so sweet, that all I can do is merely nod.

He helps me into my seat, then inclines his head at the buffet table. "Do you want me to get you something?"

"Yes, please." Lunch was more than a few hours ago.

I smooth my skirts out around me and settle in to wait, watching the laughing guests as they mill and mingle. Soon Noah returns with two glasses of red wine and two heaping plates of tapas.

"This looks great." Noah sets a plate down in front of me but before I can dig in, I hear him chuckle.

Following his gaze, I spot Rosita on the dance floor and smile, watching as she dances with her thirteen-year-old son who's taller than she is.

"What did she think about her promotion?" I ask, helping myself to a bite of grilled prawn.

With the same fondness in his eyes that a son has for a mother, Noah smiles. "She hugged me. And then when I told her the pay increase, she cried."

I place my hand over his. My sweet, loving husband is a good man underneath it all, and I know I'm blessed beyond measure.

"Looks like everyone's having a good time," I say as I raise my glass to my lips. The reception party for our not-a-wedding is in full swing.

Noah chuckles. "That's for sure. I can already tell who's going to hook up later."

"What are you talking about?"

"Oh, come on, Snowflake. You can't tell me you've never played that guessing game at weddings before."

It does sound kind of fun, but I still roll my eyes at

him. Just to tease him, I point to Sterling and Camryn, standing near the bar.

"Okay then, how much do you want to bet on them?" I ask sarcastically. No way would those two ever hook up.

Noah squints in their direction—then bursts out laughing.

"What? Are you okay?" I ask, bewildered.

"So *that's* why Sterling has seemed so restless lately. Damn, how did I not see it before? He was getting laid just like usual, but the difference was, there was a specific girl he wanted who he couldn't get. All the signs were there; I was just too wrapped up in my own shit to notice. I'll have to bring him a beer later . . . and tease him about his little crush until he punches me."

Now I'm staring toward the bar too. "Sterling and Camryn? Really?" My brain is still hung up on that part. But when my gaze falls back to Noah, I shrug, smiling. *Then again, I guess stranger stars have aligned.*

"Hey, Noah," I say softly. "I've been thinking about something. Specifically, about us . . . having a baby."

He whips around to gape at me. "What do you mean?"

I take his hand in mine. "I've thought a lot about this. Everyone said your life will change. Well, just like I always do, I had to break that down into pros versus cons. I wasn't sure I wanted our life to change. But ever since the whole heir clause thing, it's been on my mind, and after I had some time to think about it, I realized . . . I like the sound of starting a family with you." I rest my forehead against his, looking deep into the dark eyes I hold so dear. "It's more than worth it to me. And I'm not saying right away, but maybe we just see. So if you're okay with it too, I wanted you to know . . . I'm open to the possibility."

For a second, he just stares, his mouth slightly open. Then he crushes our lips together, fiery and joyful. "Are you kidding?" He gasps. "I'm crazy about you. I'm more than okay with this—I'm over the fucking moon." Another hard kiss. "I love you so much. You make me so happy." The words pour out between hot, sweet kisses, as if he can't stand to keep his emotions inside but he also can't stand to stop touching me, our guests be dammed.

I love being the center of this man's world. And even though I can't imagine that anything could top this moment, somehow I know that our wedding night will.

# Chapter Fourteen

*Olivia*

The dreamy little smile on my lips refuses to fade. The night has been magical. Enchanted. I felt like a princess. But instead of being rescued from a dark castle, my prince rescued me from a loveless life of monotony and work. With Noah by my side, everything is brighter.

The limousine drops us off at home. Rather than being tired from the late hour, I'm energized. As Noah unlocks our front door, I'm struck by how the meaning of this penthouse apartment has changed for me. Dad gave it to us as an early wedding gift, but we were only getting married in the legal sense, and at the time, I hadn't even come around to *that* idea yet. Noah and I could barely call each other friends. The gift was an awkward shock. I was angry, scared, resentful at being forced out of my own space.

For the first couple of weeks, Noah and I tiptoed around each other like houseguests. But eventually, as we grew closer, it became a comfortable refuge where we reunited at the end of a long day and restored each other's spirits. Now it's our true marital home—a place where love sprouted and took root. It's truly *ours*, truly shared, not just a lease that happens to have two names on it.

I'm startled out of my thoughts when Noah bends low and sweeps me off my feet—literally, with one strong arm under my knees and the other under my shoulders.

"W-what are you doing?" I squeak, throwing my arms around his neck.

He chuckles, and I can feel the vibration in his chest even through his tuxedo jacket. "Carrying you across the threshold. What does it look like, Snowflake?"

I relax slightly, no longer nervous about falling. "That was supposed to happen when we were first married."

"Yeah, but I didn't do it at the time. All of today is my big do-over." His voice lowers to a sultry hum.

"And that includes the wedding night we never got."

Damn, I like the sound of that. I let him know by stretching up to kiss his stubbled jaw.

Cradling me bridal-style, Noah steps easily through the doorway as if I weigh nothing. "Anywhere else you want to go while your chariot is still at your service? Like the bedroom?"

"I thought you were always at my service," I tease as I glance around. "Hmm, how about the couch first? We should relax a little before just jumping into things."

Noah carries me into the living room and sets me on the couch. But before he can straighten up again, I grip his lapels and tug him down with me, into a tangle of limbs and a deep kiss that leaves us both flushed.

"What happened to taking tonight slow?" His voice is noticeably huskier.

With the mischievous grin that I learned from him, I reply, "I lied." Then I push Noah back to sit up and swing my leg over his lap, straddling him.

He gives a quiet murmur of approval and kisses

me. I return it, and our tongues dance hard and deep. I hike up the skirt of my dress so that I can grind my hips down against his growing erection. He rewards me with another rougher growl that demands more. Without breaking our kiss, I unbutton his tuxedo jacket. He shrugs it off and tosses it toward the far end of the couch, letting it land in a heap. But when I reach down to unzip his pants, Noah catches my hand.

"Wait, babe," he says, sounding like it pains him to stop me. "Slow down; let me get a condom." He reaches for his discarded suit jacket to grab his wallet.

Now it's my turn to cover his hand with mine. "Actually, I was thinking we'd go without one tonight."

I bite my lip, grinning, when he stares at me with an earnest expression in his eyes.

"Don't fucking tease me like that, baby." He lets out a low groan. "Did you start taking the pill or something?"

"No, I'm not on any birth control." I know the words I spoke to him earlier tonight must be flashing through his mind with even greater clarity. "Tonight I'm ready to feel you, all of you. Just us . . . together."

"Fuck yes, baby, that sounds so fucking perfect."

I need him now. Working my hand into the front of his pants, I pull his cock out and stroke it while he releases a satisfied sigh.

Noah's hands go to work, unzipping the back of my dress, and I rise to my feet and watch it puddle on the floor. As soon as I step out of the dress, I plant myself back in Noah's warm lap, not wanting to stay away for even a second.

I trace the lettering I'm still getting used to, loving it more than I ever thought possible, and he inhales sharply at my touch.

"I can't believe you put my name here. It's permanent, you know?"

"So are we," he murmurs, kissing my throat.

His fingertips trace my curves, the white silky lace of my lingerie. But I can't wait any longer. I yank aside my panties and impale myself on him, sinking down onto his steely length with a satisfied sigh.

Noah bites his lip and moans deep in his chest, an animal sound of pure pleasure. "Holy fuck, that feels amazing."

I have to agree with him. Something about the sensation of his hot flesh directly against mine is so gratifying, so intimate and primal. I can feel every detail of his cock inside me—the ridge where head becomes shaft, the way it twitches when I clench my inner muscles. And even if it didn't feel any different for me, just the knowledge that his pleasure has intensified so much would be fucking hot.

He grips my ass cheeks in his palms, lifting and lowering me slowly. His biceps flex with each movement, and I feel like a goddess perched on her throne with the way he's worshiping my skin, nibbling my throat.

Time to test his stamina. I set a fast pace, riding him hard, my breath coming fast from my throat every time I plunge down and thrust his cock straight into my G-spot. Neither of us gives a shit that Noah is still mostly dressed and we haven't made it to the bedroom. This is the honeymoon we never got to have, and we're damn well going to enjoy it.

"Olivia . . ." Noah moans, as if just saying my name gives him pleasure. "I love you. You're my . . . whole world."

Words fail me. The devotion shining in his eyes is too much—I can barely breathe, let alone speak. I crush our mouths together, trying to pour all my happiness into my kiss, knowing he'll understand. This man is all mine. He chased me, caught me, tattooed my name on his skin, and now I'm never letting go.

The sounds of panting and the smack of skin on skin fill the air. I gasp when Noah's hand pushes between our sweaty, writhing bodies to start working my clit. He bucks his hips to meet me with every thrust, his other arm locked tight around my waist to keep up the demanding rhythm. He alternately cranes his head up to kiss me or down to bury his face in my breasts, licking and sucking my nipples.

"Come for me," Noah growls, rubbing my clit harder. "You're so beautiful. Let me make you come, let me watch you . . ."

I've never wanted anything so bad. Feverishly I grind down on him, needing more, faster. I've been waiting all day to touch him like this. The heat between my legs coils tight—

Then finally snaps, flooding white sparks of pleasure throughout my body. My arms tighten around him, every muscle quivering in ecstasy as I fall into his dark, adoring eyes.

"So perfect," Noah pants. "I can feel you coming, pulsing around me . . ." His words dissolve into a loud groan and his cock throbs inside me.

It feels like forever until the tremors fade. With his cock still softening in me, I rest my sweaty forehead against Noah's. He kisses me softly, just the barest brush of lips.

When I've caught my breath, I lean back to brush a stray curl of damp hair out of his eyes, smiling down at him fondly. Noah has spiced up my life in ways I never could have anticipated. I'm happier, calmer, more carefree and adventurous. And not just because of the increase in orgasms, either . . . although that certainly doesn't hurt.

I feel a dripping sensation between my thighs. My smile falters and my cheeks flush when I realize it's Noah's come. I've never had condom-less sex with a man before. Obviously, I knew it would involve him coming inside me, but actually *feeling* the evidence is a totally different matter. It's both embarrassing and strangely, unexpectedly hot.

Noah reads my mind. "Want me to clean you up?"

That sounds nice . . . also really hot, actually. "You got me all messy, so it only seems fair," I tease my sweet husband.

Noah rises, lifting me into his arms, and carries me toward the bedroom. I bury my face in the crook of his neck, a sigh of love on my lips.

# Epilogue

*Olivia*

*Three Months Later*

I close my laptop with a sigh. It's five o'clock on the dot. Normally, I might be tempted to work overtime, but not today. My Monday, Wednesday, and Friday evenings are reserved for visiting Dad. My younger sister, Rachel, visits him on Tuesday and Thursday afternoons, since her classes end early on those days, and she often spends weekends with him too.

Dad's health has declined steadily ever since he fell the night of Tate & Cane's gala. Our Hail Mary pass, the night that saved our company, also spelled the beginning of his end. Three months ago, Dad was given only one more month to live. His doctors aren't really sure how he exceeded that prognosis by such a huge margin—although Dad himself always says, "It's because my two wonderful daughters visit so often and keep my spirits up."

But it's clear that his journey will come to an end soon; we just don't know exactly when. He's confined to his bed much of the time, but he has a helpful staff to look after him in his own home, rather than in a hospital.

Not too long ago, I thought I'd be sobbing nonstop. And sometimes I do still find myself choking up. But Dad is so positive about everything that I can't help being soothed. His lack of fear and his acceptance of his death has helped me accept it too. I try to cherish the present moment instead of mourning the inevitable and letting it spoil what little time we have left. Whenever the tears come, I let myself feel them, but with hope that the grief doesn't pull me under completely.

My car purrs as I leave New York City behind, away from its noisy, smoggy hustle into the slower quiet of the suburbs. Instead of pulling my car into his garage when I arrive, I park on the street outside the front gate and walk up the winding driveway, enjoying the crisp air of the last days of autumn. The garden's flowers have faded and fallen, but their leaves are still green, the rosebushes are still pregnant with plump red blooms. The oak tree sheltering the house is a blaze of orange and yellow.

I let myself in the front door. A woman in scrubs bustles past me down the main hall. I recognize her as the registered nurse who comes once a day to monitor Dad's condition. I walk to the master bedroom, which has been transformed into a makeshift hospital room: a mechanized bed, a wheelchair, an IV stand, an oxygen tank, a host of gently beeping monitors. Another younger woman in plainclothes—his overnight aide who sleeps in the guest bedroom—peers at me over the top of the book she's reading. The sight of all this medical equipment is still a little intimidating, but it reassures me to know that someone is here to help him at all hours.

"Hi, Dad. How are you feeling?" I say as I cross the room. Dad is sitting up in bed. *Today must be a relatively pain-free day.*

He raises his hand in a weak wave, a cluster of tubes and wires trailing from his arm. "Good afternoon, sweetheart. Tell me how you are first."

I smile at him. He always insists upon that, no matter what. I lean down to kiss his cheek and sit in the armchair by his side.

"Well, Tate & Cane is doing great. Our stock prices are higher than they've been in ten years. We've been getting so many work offers, we've actually had to hire a few freelance subcontractors to pick up the slack."

"Excellent news," he says. "I'm so proud of you and Noah. You two kids have done more for this company than I ever dreamed. I only wish Bill had lived to see this day, but I suppose I'll just have to tell him all about it when I get to heaven." Then he gives me a pointed look, his thinning eyebrows slightly raised. "Do you enjoy being a CEO? I hope you've been taking enough time for yourself too."

"Yes, I love it. And we try to reserve weekends for relaxing together."

"Sounds like things are pleasant at home."

I nod, grinning. Sometimes I still get giddy over the fact that I'm married to Noah—happily now, not just legally. "And I have a big announcement."

"Oh?"

I lean over to take Dad's hand and look him in the eye. "I'm pregnant."

Joy dawns gradually over his face as the good news sinks in. "Really? You're sure?"

"I just went to the doctor yesterday for an official test." Usually, it's not a great idea to announce a pregnancy so early, but a grandchild is my father's dying wish. I can jump the gun a little bit.

"Oh, how wonderful." He heaves a blissful sigh and there are tears shimmering in his eyes.

It's a moment I wasn't sure I'd ever get to have with my father, and it's every bit as sweet and heartfelt as I imagined it would be.

"How are you feeling? And have you thought about names yet?" he asks.

"I'm feeling great; don't worry. We figured William or Frederick for a boy, Dahlia or Susan for a girl." It only seems right to name our baby after one of its grandparents.

Dad blinks, then laughs until a coughing fit cuts him off. "I appreciate the thought, sweetheart, but for God's sake, don't name the poor thing Fred. Or at least use it for the middle, not the first. That name is getting to be on the old-fashioned side these days."

I give him a look. "And Dahlia isn't?"

"Perhaps, but you'll have to take that up with Noah."

"I'll keep that in mind," I say with a chuckle. Without letting go of Dad's hand, I pull a small, folded square of cloth from my purse. "But I'm not sure he'll be able to think straight for a few days. He was so excited yesterday, he ran right out of the doctor's office and bought this."

Dad unfolds the present. It's an infant onesie made of butter-soft, pale yellow cotton. Beaming at me, he hugs the tiny piece of clothing to his heart.

I gently squeeze his free hand. "Okay, Dad, I told you how I've been. Now you tell me how you are."

"Do you even need to ask, sweetheart? I couldn't be happier."

Blinking back tears, I reply simply, "Me too."

# Epilogue Two

*Noah*

I did it. I totally put a bun in her oven. I am so the fucking man. My wife is incredible, and I can't wait to see her as a mother. Because this baby? This will make us a true family, and one I'm honored to be part of.

Even sweeter news? In an unexpected twist, we learned from Prescott that the estate attorney over my father's will had been instructed not to tell us that the will had stipulated our shares of the company be placed in a trust if the heir clause wasn't met within ninety days, but if we did marry and produce an heir at a later date, the shares would revert to our child. It's an even happier happy ending. We've got this.

*Game on.*

# Coming Soon

## The Fix Up

British bad boy Sterling Quinn needs a wife.

After his great-grandfather, the former prince something or another, passes and leaves him millions, Sterling is shocked to discover the massive inheritance has a clause—he needs to clean up his image and be married in order to receive his millions.

When word gets out that this hottie has royal blood running through his veins and is on the prowl for Mrs. Right, crazy ex-girlfriends, schoolyard crushes, and thousands of other hopeful women flock to his doorstep. What he needs is a manager to help him sort through the clutter.

Enter Camryn Palmer, PR executive.

Camryn has had a front-row seat to her friend Sterling's revolving door of a love life for years. But when she's hired to clean up his image, and manage the hordes of women cruising through his bedroom door, she's stuck between a rock and a hard place.

*Literally.*

Yes, she has secret fantasies about being the one to keep his bed warm, but what woman doesn't? He's sinfully attractive and she wants to kiss that cocky English accent right off his lips, but she's got a job to do. She's a professional through and through, and besides, an arranged marriage could never be a happy one. *Right?*

Filled with hot and humorous moments, you won't want to miss *The Fix Up*!

# Acknowledgments

I would like to thank the following ladies who played an important role in helping me bring *Hitched* into the world: Alexandra Fresch, Hang Le, Natasha Gentile, Rachel Brookes, Danielle Sanchez, and Pam Berehulke. I'm so grateful to have each of you on my team.

A big thank-you to Crystal Patriarche and the BookSparks Team. I'd like to give a shout-out to the Cuties in my private Facebook Group, Kendall's Kinky Cuties, and say thank you for cheering me on and being my go-to place when I want to steal a few minutes away and hang out online.

And to John. Always John.

# About the Author

A *New York Times*, *Wall Street Journal*, and *USA TODAY* bestselling author of more than twenty titles, Kendall Ryan has sold more than a million e-books, and her books have been translated into several languages in countries around the world. She's a traditionally published author with Simon & Schuster and Harper Collins UK, as well as an independently published author.

Since she first began self-publishing in 2012, she's appeared at #1 on Barnes & Noble and iBooks charts around the world. Her books have also appeared on the *New York Times* and *USA TODAY* bestseller list more than two dozen times. Ryan has been featured in such publications as *USA TODAY*, *Newsweek*, and *In Touch Weekly*.

Visit her at:

www.kendallryanbooks.com

# Other Books by Kendall Ryan

UNRAVEL ME Series:
*Unravel Me*
*Make Me Yours*

LOVE BY DESIGN Series:
*Working It*
*Craving Him*
*All or Nothing*

WHEN I BREAK Series:
*When I Break*
*When I Surrender*
*When We Fall*

FILTHY BEAUTIFUL LIES Series:
*Filthy Beautiful Lies*
*Filthy Beautiful Love*
*Filthy Beautiful Lust*
*Filthy Beautiful Forever*

LESSONS WITH THE DOM Series:

*The Gentleman Mentor*

*Sinfully Mine*


ALPHAS UNDONE Series:

*Bait & Switch*

*Slow & Steady*


IMPERFECT LOVE Series:

*Hitched Volume 1*

*Hitched Volume 2*

*Hitched Volume 3*


STAND-ALONE NOVELS:

*Hard to Love*

*Reckless Love*

*Resisting Her*

*The Impact of You*

*Screwed*

*Monster Prick*